# Trouble on Tuesday

## Colleen L. Reece

A Barbour Book

# Trouble on Tuesday

© MCMXCVII by Barbour & Company, Inc.

ISBN 1-55748-984-X

Published by Barbour & Company, Inc.
        P.O. Box 719
        Uhrichsville, Ohio  44683
        http://www.barbourbooks.com

 Member of the
Evangelical Christian
Publishers Association

Printed in the United States of America.

# CHAPTER 1

Dark-haired Shannon Riley yawned and turned to face her best friend, Juli Scott, snuggled beneath the yellow comforter in the matching twin bed in Juli's room. Her gray-blue Irish eyes sparkled with fun. "After all the excitement, starting with your *Mysterious Monday* (Juli Scott, Super Sleuth, Book One), going back to school tomorrow is going to be hard," she complained.

"I'm just glad it's all over." Juli shivered and slid deeper under the covers. Her light brown hair with golden highlights spilled onto her pillow and made her dark-blue eyes look enormous. "All those long months of wondering if I belonged on a funny farm for believing Dad wasn't dead, then the drug bust. . ." Juli's voice trailed off and she stared at Shannon. "If you hadn't been there for me, I don't know what I'd have done."

"Mercy me, why would you be for thinkin' I wouldn't?" came the indignant answer.

Juli groaned. "Excuse me. Any time you go into that Irish accent of yours I know it's time to change the subject."

"People from Ireland do have Irish accents." Shannon smirked.

"Then how come you only use yours when you're trying to send me a message?" Juli teased. "Most of the time you talk like the rest of us, except when you quote—actually, *mis*quote—clichés no one else would be caught dead using. The worst thing is, you have half the sophomore class at Hillcrest using Rileyisms instead of speaking English!"

"Love me, love my accent," Shannon misquoted. Juli had the feeling this time she'd done it on purpose. "It doesn't stop me from being number one assistant to Ms. Juli Scott, Bellingham, Washington's own super sleuth." Shannon cocked her head to one side. "Or is that spot reserved for a tall basketball player named Dave Gilmore? He's the one who wound up getting his face bruised when he defended you and your dad." She opened her eyes wide. "Wonder how he will explain it at school? We were warned not to talk about what happened at Skagit House, but the kids will ask."

Juli groaned and the corners of her mouth turned down. "Especially Amy Hilton. She makes such a big deal out of everything. I can just hear her." Juli slipped into a reasonable imitation of the tiny, blond cheerleader's voice:

" 'Ooooh, Dave, your poor face! What happened?' "

Shannon giggled appreciatively. "Dave's doing great at getting away from Amy. Does love make people more courageous?"

"Love! Don't be stupid." Juli felt a hot blush rise from the collar of her sleepshirt. "Dave Gilmore didn't start paying attention to girls until this year." She couldn't help the grin that spread across her face. "I have to admit, I'm glad he started with me."

"So am I. He's almost as nice as Ted Hilton."

"Nicer," Juli shot back. "For starters, Dave doesn't have a bratty twin sister named Amy. Ted does."

"Don't remind me," Shannon mumbled. "I made a be-nice-to-Amy-if-humanly-possible New Year's resolution." She yawned again. "Does Dave have any brothers or sisters? I don't remember him talking about them."

"That could be because most of the time we've been busy chasing brown vans and shadowy men," Juli reminded. "I think he has a little sister named Christy, about eight or nine." She punched up her pillow, patted her cinnamon-brown plush teddy bear Clue, who sat on her desk next to her bed, and switched off the bedside light. "It's getting late. See you tomorrow."

A sleepy "uh-huh" came from the other bed, then silence.

Juli closed her eyes. It felt so good to know Mom *and* Dad lay sleeping in the master bedroom. A flood threatened to leak from the dam behind her eyelids. For the dozenth time, she prayed the prayer that had pounded the walls of her heart for the past few days. "Thank You so much, God, for bringing Dad home and taking care of us all. Please forgive me for doubting. All those awful months, feeling You'd moved away when I needed You the most, are over. It's Monday again. Dad's home. Mom's walking around like she just won the lottery, and I've never been happier in my life. Thanks again. In Jesus' name. Amen."

She shifted position until she lay curled like a kitten. Tomorrow she'd see Dave: before school, between classes, maybe in the cafeteria. That by itself was enough to make it a terrific Tuesday, although the day following a three-day weekend normally dragged. *I think I'll wear my new blue sweater,* Juli planned. Before she had thought through the rest of an outfit, she fell asleep.

"Weather prediction: clear and cold," Gary Scott announced the next morning at breakfast in the dining room. Sunlight streamed in on blooming house plants. Window sun-catchers made rainbows on the pale green walls. It reminded Juli so much of the day he left and didn't come home, she had to swallow hard to get her juice down.

Dad eyed Mom, trim in the scarlet pants suit her first-graders loved. "You look a little strange without your HOME-MAKER FIRST CLASS sweatshirt. Cute, though."

"Cute!" Juli objected. "She looks great, super, fantastic. . ."

Dad threw his hands in the air. "Okay, okay. I just miss her the way she was." He quickly added, "That doesn't mean I'm not proud of her, of you both. The way you carried on while I was gone was spectacular."

"Mom, will you continue teaching?" Shannon asked, with the assurance that came from being considered Anne Scott's "second daughter."

"For the rest of the year, at least. We'll need a family conference before we decide about the future." Joy radiated in every movement. "Right now, I'm not sure I can settle down enough to get through even one more day." She hastily brushed moisture from her lashes and smiled unsteadily at her husband.

The look Dad gave her in return showed Juli the depth and strength of her parents' love for one another. A quick glance at Shannon showed she felt the same way. She'd told Juli shortly after they met how deeply her parents Sean and Katie had cared for each other. "They were even more in love the day Mother died than when they married," Shannon had quietly said.

*That's the way I want it to be for me,* Juli thought. She felt herself blush. Why should Dave Gilmore's twinkling blue eyes come to mind? She'd date a bunch of people before she finished college and considered marriage. So would he. Funny. Telling herself that didn't help a bit when she caught a glimpse of Dave down the hall before the bell rang for her first class. Juli secretly felt glad he hadn't seen her and her tomato-red face.

Contrary to Shannon and Juli's predictions, Amy didn't comment on Dave's bruised face. At lunch, she waltzed into the cafeteria and over to the table where some of the kids from the church youth group usually sat. Parking her tray down in the empty space next to John Foster—her quiet, on-again, off-again boyfriend—she caroled, "Guess what!" She waved a page from a newspaper. "My horoscope says today is my lucky day." Her light blue eyes shone with anticipation. "Wonder what wonderful thing will happen?"

"You don't believe that stuff, do you?" Juli asked. "It's canned. Not long ago I saw an advertisement in a magazine asking for people to write horoscopes."

"Really?" Amy looked thrilled. "Are you going to apply?"

"No way. It's world class dumb." Juli peered at the rest of her limp spaghetti and decided she'd had enough.

The petite blond acted disappointed. "You should. Except I thought they studied the stars and stuff like that before they wrote horoscopes."

"Don't get mixed up in that stuff," her brother Ted warned. "Remember what our pastor said about dabbling in the occult."

Amy stared at him. "Occult!" Her tinkly little laugh rang out. "It's just for fun. Besides, what does it hurt if I believe this is going to be my lucky day? If I believe hard enough, maybe I can make it happen. Doesn't the Bible say we should believe when we pray?"

"Better stick with the Bible, instead of relying on some fake fortune," Ted advised. "Give it to me and I'll toss it in the garbage where it belongs."

Amy held it out of reach. "No! I want to read fortunes for the rest of you."

"Not me," Juli put in.

"Or me," Dave, John, and Ted agreed.

To Juli's surprise, Shannon smiled at Amy and said, "You can read mine, Amy." Was this response motivated by her New Year's resolution to be nice to Amy? Juli choked on her brownie and hastily swallowed a mouthful of milk.

The blond girl absolutely beamed. "When's your birthday?"

"January twenty-fifth, just a week after Juli's."

"How come you didn't tell us?" Ted demanded.

"If you remember, we've been pretty busy." Shannon sent him a warning look. "It's neat being sixteen. Driver's license soon, and Dad's getting me a car."

The magic word *car* captured the boys' attention. "What kind? If you need help picking one out, we're available," they solemnly assured her.

"Especially me," Ted added, with a mischievous grin.

"Forget cars and listen, will you?" Amy shook the paper threateningly in their direction, then ran a highly polished fingernail down the printed horoscope. "Here it is. *'Beware of those who offer help. They may not be trustworthy.'* " Shannon stared at Amy. A shout of laughter rose from the table, so loud it caused the entire cafeteria to look their way. "Of all the coincidences!" Laughter bubbled from Shannon like a geyser. "You boys tell me you'll help me find a car. Ten seconds later, the horoscope warns me not to trust you!"

*Why don't I think it's funny?* Juli wondered. *It's just a dumb horoscope. Like Shannon said, it's also pure coincidence.* Yet for some reason she couldn't join in the fun, even when a hot argument followed, with Amy triumphantly pointing out how well the fortune fit.

For the rest of the day, Juli fought the knowledge that her terrific Tuesday had been spoiled. No matter how often she told herself she was acting silly, she couldn't get rid of the feeling. To make things worse, she came close to quarreling with Shannon on the bus ride home—something they'd never done in all the months since they started their sophomore year together and became instant friends.

They climbed on the bus and the friendly driver gave his usual worn-out greeting, "Glad to see you two together. One without the other's like—"

"—ham without eggs," they automatically finished. Juli had barely sat down before she burst out, "I wish Amy had left her old horoscope home."

"Why?" Shannon looked surprised.

"You don't believe it was anything but coincidence, do you?" Juli cried.

"Not really, but you have to admit it was funny." She giggled. "So was the expression on the boys' faces."

Juli refused to be sidetracked. "It's just plain stupid."

"Lighten up, Juli. A horoscope is just words on paper."

"So was Hitler's book that told people to hate the Jews," Juli said sourly.

Shannon looked shocked. "It's not the same thing at all," she began. When her friend maintained a stormy silence, she slowly said, "Maybe we'd better not talk about it. I don't understand why you're so upset, but it isn't worth arguing over."

Relieved without understanding why, Juli put her hand on Shannon's arm. "I don't know why I am, either. We kid around a lot, but I don't want to argue with you. Ever." Nameless fear made her fingers tighten on Shannon's parka sleeve before she pulled them away. The same unexplainable fear slowed her steps on the way home from the bus stop after Shannon turned the other way. Nothing must come between her and Shannon, especially a senseless quarrel about something connected with Amy. She'd simply forget her and her horoscope.

The next day at the bus stop, Shannon was no different than ever. Juli gave a secret sigh of relief. Following the "ham and eggs" routine, they chattered about school and church activities, homework, and the basketball team. Shannon didn't mention Amy. Neither did Juli. She felt thoroughly ashamed at having allowed herself to get so disturbed by absolutely nothing that she had risked quarreling with her best friend. At least the incident was behind her.

Wrong. The girls no sooner got off the bus and inside the doors of Hillcrest High than Ted Hilton raced up to them. "Wait 'til you hear about Amy!"

"Hear what?"

"She's not sick, is she?"

"Sick?" Ted snorted and his blue eyes flashed. "She's just inherited a bundle of money, *enough to buy a brand-new sports car.*"

"You're kidding!" Shannon gasped.

Speechless, Juli dropped her books. She made no effort to retrieve them, just stood there staring at Ted as if she had never seen him before.

"Do I look like I'm kidding?" Ted demanded. "Hey, Amy, come over here," he bellowed down the hall.

One look at the flying figure confirmed the incredible news. Amy Hilton had certainly inherited something. "Did you tell them?" she demanded.

"Yeah, but they don't believe it." Ted grinned. It didn't detract from the excitement that surrounded him and his sister like fog off Bellingham Bay.

"It's true. Some great-aunt I barely knew existed, except that I was named for her, put me in her will," Amy babbled. Her short blond curls bounced up and down with every movement of her body.

"What's happening?" Dave Gilmore's voice came over Juli's shoulder.

She turned. "Amy just inherited some money."

"I told you the horoscope wasn't a fake," the cheerleader crowed. "It said yesterday was my lucky day and it was!"

Juli clenched her fingers. She wanted to shriek that it was still coincidence, but what good would it do? The expressions on the faces of those who had gathered around Amy ranged from outright disbelief, to wonder, to acceptance. Nothing she could say would change the opinion of those who wanted to believe in such things.

She turned to Shannon, expecting to find a raised eyebrow, or the same skeptical look John Foster wore. To Juli's horror, her best friend in the whole world, except for God, looked as eager and willing to believe Amy's claim as many of the others!

# CHAPTER 2

Juli wrote in her journal a few days later:

*I've discovered why mystery writers always leave you up in the air at the end of a chapter or right after an exciting scene. It's because life is that way. The kids at school are still talking about Amy and her horoscope. Shannon doesn't say a word. I don't, either. It feels strange not to be able to share things with her, almost as bad as when I knew secrets but was ordered to keep quiet about them.*

Juli stopped writing long enough to glance at Clue. His shiny dark eyes stared right back at her. "You're all right," she told him. "You just sit there patiently waiting until I pay you some attention. I can say anything to you and know you won't get your feelings hurt. You never judge me, either." She grinned. "Even when I carry on a one-way conversation with a stuffed bear!"

A trace of the grin remained when she went on writing.

*Amy's getting her car this weekend. I wanted to laugh when she let on she decided it was dumb to spend all her money on a car. Ted had already told Shannon their parents said "Absolutely not!" when Amy started picking out cars to die for. Most of the money will be saved for her college expenses. Her folks did agree to a bright red Mustang convertible one of their friends wanted to sell. Just what she needs to increase her popularity.*

Juli hastily crossed out the last sentence. She couldn't help being envious of Amy and her new car. Putting it down in a journal would remind her every time she went back and read what she'd written. Who needed that?

In its place she wrote:

*Sorry, Lord. I'm working on trying to like her better, but it's sure hard! Thanks for understanding, and forgiving me. You know I have good intentions.*

"Actions speak louder than talking about them," Shannon had misquoted once when they were discussing Amy.

"It's 'speak louder than words,' " Juli had told her.

"Words, talking, whatever." She airily waved away Juli's correction. "I do wish Amy would make it easier by not acting so phony."

Now Juli grinned and added:

*Can't wait for the youth Valentine Banquet at church. Wonder what kind of decorations Amy and her committee came up with? Shannon and I are going with Ted and Dave. Wonder if they'll send us corsages?*

The boys did. Juli's white sweetheart roses looked great against a new turquoise dress that made her eyes look bluer than ever. Shannon's red roses nestled against soft cream that set off her dark hair and ivory skin.

When they reached the church and stepped into the Fellowship Hall, the girls gasped. Amy and her committee had outdone themselves. The room looked so much like a cross between fairyland and a snow palace with icicles, it made Juli homesick for the Skagit House. Silvery flakes sprinkled on the floor made even it look wintry. Concealed spotlights shed rose, green, orchid, and amber streams until it felt like they were in the middle of a crystal rainbow. Shiny red hearts provided just enough color to carry out the Valentine's Day theme.

"Do you like it?" an eager voice asked.

Juli whirled. Amy, wearing a sophisticated black dress

more appropriate to a cocktail party than a church banquet, stood just behind her. "It's absolutely gorgeous!" The pleasure in the other girl's face surprised Juli. Maybe Shannon was right when she said sometimes she felt sorry for Amy, who always tried too hard when she really didn't need to. Like wearing clothes that didn't leave enough to the imagination and smiling into her date's eyes as if he were the only boy in the room.

"I wouldn't be caught dead and buried in that dress," Shannon whispered in Juli's ear. Juli didn't bother to correct her.

The sound of laughter to the right caught the group's attention. The smile faded from Amy's face. For an instant, misery filled her eyes.

"Hi, everyone." John Foster came toward them, accompanied by a red-haired girl with warm brown eyes and what Ted Hilton called a "speckled" (meaning freckled) face. "Do you all know Molly Bowen?"

"Kind of." Juli smiled at the newcomer. "You're a new sophomore, aren't you? I'm glad you've started coming to the youth group."

Before Molly could answer, Amy cut in. "Hello, John. This is Brett." She nodded toward her date and gave John a dazzling smile.

"Hi." He smiled, then turned his attention back to Molly. "It must be time to find our places. Nice job, Amy." John took Molly's arm and walked off.

Amy's face turned bright red, then she laughed. "Come

on, Brett. We're at the head table." She led him away.

Ted broke the uncomfortable silence. "John deserves a girl like Molly. The sad thing is, Amy probably likes him better than anyone else, but she went too far. She insisted they bring her new Mustang tonight. John refused, so she got Brett to bring her. I hope this teaches her a lesson." He shrugged. "Forget it. This is a party, right?"

"Right!" the others joined in.

"Almost as beautiful as up at Skagit House," Dave said after they found their places and he seated Juli.

"I was just thinking the same thing."

"Something else we have in common." The changing lights made his smooth hair shine. "It's amazing what people can do with decorating. I have to admit, I like the outdoors better, even though this is really something. Nature's free so everyone can enjoy it, not just a bunch of people who come to a church banquet. Know what I mean?" He sounded a little anxious.

"I do," Juli enthusiastically agreed.

"Careful how you throw those words around," Dave teased.

She felt glad for the changing colors and hoped they hid the blush that brought warmth to her face. Her heart also gave a little bounce. No way did she want things to get heavy and spoil what she called the "simple joy of being together." Yet his teasing and admiration added extra sparkle to the romantic decorations. Tomorrow they'd go back to jeans and ski sweaters, boots and thick socks. Just for tonight they were a different Dave and Juli.

After dinner, Pastor Johnson gave a short talk, beginning with, "I promised not to preach!" When the laughter died, he said, "The roots of Valentine's Day go deep. There are many conflicting reports as to how it started. My favorite is about an early Christian named Valentine, a man loved by children. According to the story, he refused to worship the Roman gods, so they put him in prison. The children missed Valentine so much, they tossed loving notes between the bars of his prison window. February 14 was named St. Valentine's Day by Pope Gelasius, in A.D. 496. Over the years, the custom of sending valentines to show love and friendship became common."

He stopped and smiled. "The greatest valentine in the world is the Bible. In it, God sends His message of love and salvation to all who will listen. I hope each year as you celebrate this special day, you will take time to thank God, Author of the first real love messages."

Tears sparkled in Shannon's long, dark lashes. Her expression when she turned Juli's way spoke more clearly than words. Any misunderstanding that had existed, even in Juli's mind, vanished in the look they exchanged.

Juli floated up the walk when Dave took her home, totally happy and at peace with the world and everyone in it. On the dimly lit porch, Dave put his hands on her shoulders. "How'd you like to be my girlfriend?"

Stunned, she couldn't answer. Was he serious? She'd secretly thought he was the greatest for so long, but she didn't think he had acted *that* interested.

When she didn't reply, Dave's hands dropped. "Like I said, we have a lot in common. Besides, I didn't mean forever." His laugh didn't sound normal. "Remember when we went sledding and you teased me with all that stuff on Shakespeare? I thought you might think about being my girlfriend *pro tem*."

"Which means, 'For the time being,' right?" she translated. "I—I'd love to."

"You would?" He hugged Juli, then his cold cheek touched hers. He dropped a quick kiss on her lips, warm and a little shy. "See you tomorrow."

"See you," Juli echoed. She watched him head to the Mustang, climb in, and drive away. A feeling of joy swept through her. After she told Mom and Dad about the banquet, she crawled into bed. For once, Juli was glad Shannon hadn't stayed over. She needed to write in her journal.

*I must be kind of old-fashioned, but there really is something to be said for not kissing every boy you go out with. I get the feeling Dave's experience may be as limited as mine. I'm glad. Tonight was so nice. I don't mean straight out of a romance novel. It was actually more like a wonderful feeling that someone thinks I'm special. Shannon will laugh about my being Dave's girlfriend pro tem. I'm not going to tell her—or anyone—about the kiss. I have a feeling if I do, it will give away some of the specialness.*

The day after the Valentine Banquet, Shannon hiked the few blocks between the Rileys two-story brick home and the yellow ranch style Scott house, with its white shutters. She parked on Juli's extra twin bed and inquired, "So, how did you like the banquet?"

"Great! You?" Her lips twitched. Unless she was terribly mistaken, Juli Scott wasn't the only girl who'd been kissed good night after the Valentine Banquet.

"Great!" They went into peals of laughter, understanding each other without saying a single, betraying word.

"I feel sorry for Amy, even though she brought it on herself," Juli said.

"So do I." Shannon's eyes looked more gray than blue. "It hurts Ted for her to be like she is. Not that he says a lot. I can just tell."

"I've decided to join your be-nicer-to-Amy campaign," Juli impulsively said. "See what a good example you've set for me?"

"Of course. Don't I always?" Shannon innocently asked, but her eyes danced.

Juli threw a pillow at her and changed the subject by announcing she was now Dave Gilmore's girlfriend *pro tem.*

Shannon sat up on the bed. "Really? Since when? Oh, last night, of course."

"Uh-huh." Juli tried to control her widening grin and failed miserably. "How about you and Ted?"

"I think he'd like me to go steady. I want to and I don't," Shannon confessed. "I like Ted a lot, but I like to do other things, too. Some of the girls who go steady never have time for anyone else. I can't imagine being like them."

"Me, either." Juli leaned back and stared at the ceiling. "I don't think Dave expects that. At least, I hope not." She flipped over and looked at Shannon. "I need time to write, and time for you, and—"

"Thanks a lot for putting me first!" The corners of Shannon's mouth turned down, but her eyes twinkled. "I suppose second violin is the price I have to pay for being a someday-famous-author's friend."

"Of course, even though it's 'second fiddle,' not 'second violin'!" Juli put on a smug look. "Will it help if I promise to dedicate my first book to you with the usual, 'I could never have done it without her' tribute?"

"Maybe." Shannon leaned back on the pillows again. "How is your entry for the writing contest coming?"

Juli grimaced. "It isn't. I keep trying to do what Mrs. Sorenson says and write what I know, but that's the trouble. What do I know?" She shook her head regretfully. "If I could tell all the things that have happened in the last year I might have a chance. I can't, for a lot of reasons, including security."

"Don't give up. You'll think of something. You always come through."

"Usually at the last minute," Juli complained. "I don't want to blow this opportunity. The magazine holding the contest for unpublished young adult writers is offering a five hundred dollar cash prize for the top story, plus publication. They also seriously consider the other stories for publication at their regular rates. I'd be happy if I even made the cut and got into final consideration." She fell silent for a moment. "Are you going to enter?"

"I don't know. Should I? I like doing the assignments for our honors writing class, but I can't see myself ever becoming an author, the way you will."

Shannon's faith in Juli's ability brought a smile. "Thanks. Why not try? Who knows? You might be the one who wins." A sinking feeling inside Juli didn't stop her from being fair. "You're an excellent writer, especially about Ireland." She paused. "Do you ever get homesick? For Ireland, I mean?"

"Sometimes." Shannon's voice sounded troubled. "I know if I went back things wouldn't be the same now that Mother's gone. Yet once in a while I wake up after a dream about the way it was years ago and feel sad. Not so much for Ireland as for my childhood and growing-up years. For a few minutes, I feel like a wishbone stretched across the Atlantic Ocean. Then I thank God He brought Grand and my father and me to Washington. Did you ever think that if it hadn't happened exactly the way it did, we'd never have met?"

"It's scary thinking how just one decision can change

everything," Juli agreed.

Shannon reluctantly slid from the bed and stood. "We're getting too serious for the day after Valentine's Day. Besides, it's time for me to go start dinner. Dad will be home soon." She opened the door, stepped into the hall, then stuck her head back in. Mischief highlighted every inch of her face. "Don't dream of Dave too much," she warned. "You have a story to write." She pulled the door shut behind her just as Juli fired off another pillow in her direction.

A week later, Amy Hilton did a total about-face. She caught up with Juli in the hall at school after Shannon had gone to her class. "I want to give Shannon a belated surprise birthday party. Will you help?"

"Sure." Juli tried not to sound surprised. Evidently Shannon's being nice to Amy was paying off. "What do you have in mind?"

"A lot. We can let on there's a youth group meeting at your house, then have it called off at the last minute, after Shannon's already there. You'll walk home with her and the rest of us will be waiting. Okay?"

"Sounds fine," Juli replied. Yet after Amy left and she walked to class, the same funny feeling shot through her that had attacked the day Amy read Shannon's horoscope: *"Beware of those who offer help. They may not be trustworthy."* In spite of her warm sweater and jeans, Juli felt cold, both inside and out.

# CHAPTER 3

"What's with you and Amy?" Shannon asked at the bus stop a few mornings later. "I never thought I'd see you two closer than Burmese twins."

"Siamese." Juli stalled for time.

Shannon grinned maddeningly. "Okay. Is it all part of your be-nice-to-Amy week?"

"Not really. She asked me to help plan a youth group committee meeting. It's going to be at my house Thursday night. You're invited for dinner. Dad's the cook." A little frown crossed Juli's face. "I'll be glad when the doctor says Dad can go back to work. He's ready to climb the walls, waiting for his shoulder to heal."

"Tell me about it." Shannon rolled her eyes. "When my father is off work for more than a day or two, it's like living with a caged beast."

"I can't wait to tell him you think he's a beast," Juli teased. "Hey, how's your car hunt coming?"

Shannon made a face. "We now have enough literature on cars to insulate our house! Dad's as bad as Ted, always bringing home more information." She did an Irish jig on the sidewalk, to the amusement of the other passengers waiting for the bus. "One thing's for sartin, I'll be for havin' a fine car when they're through fillin' my head with knowledge. No blarney."

Juli groaned, then giggled. "Question: How is your Irish accent like a ghost? Answer: Now you see it, now you don't!"

Shannon looked at her suspiciously. "How do you see an accent?"

"See, hear, whatever." Juli waved the unimportant detail aside, the same way Shannon did when someone corrected her Rileyisms.

"That is so bad," her friend loftily told her, but when those around them couldn't help laughing, she joined in.

On Thursday night, Gary and Anne Scott kept Shannon too busy talking to notice the time. *Leave it to them to come through,* Juli thought. She glanced at the phone, willing it to ring. Five minutes later, she dove for the instrument. "Hello? Really? Okay."

"Now that is what I call an intelligent conversation," her father solemnly said after she hung up.

Juli wasn't about to lie, so she chose her words carefully.

"The kids on the committee aren't going to be able to come here." *The key word being "here,"* she silently praised herself.

Shannon glanced at the clock. "I can't believe they'd wait until eight o'clock to tell you. Not very considerate. If you don't mind, I'll head for home. My homework's done, but Dad said the other day he wished we could spend more time together. I'll call him." She started for the phone.

Juli nearly panicked. "No! I mean, we'll walk you home. Right, Mom? Dad?"

Dad unfolded his long legs from the footrest of his chair. "Good idea. I'm getting fat on my own cooking. Of course, that's because I only like to cook pasta dishes."

"Fat chance," Juli jeered, looking at her trim, muscular dad. "Sorry," she added when the others groaned at her unintentional pun. "It's just that fat's the last thing Dad will ever be." She hurried to the hall closet for her Christmas ski jacket, yellow with black trim. Shannon slid into her jacket, matching except red where Juli's was yellow. Although the weather had turned warmer, even the slightest February breeze off the bay blew cold.

All the way to the Rileys' two-story brick home, with its carved front door and many-paned windows, Juli wondered if Shannon would really be surprised. *Not if the kids aren't smart enough to park their cars out of sight,* she decided. *Especially Amy. That red Mustang convertible is a dead giveaway.* She pulled her jacket closer. Why should that common expression—"dead giveaway"—send a chill through her? *It must be tied to all the excitement Shannon and I have gone through.*

"Dad must not be home," Shannon said in a disappointed voice when they reached her dimly lit home. "He's a turn-on-every-light-in-the-house person."

"We'll go in with you to make sure everything's all right," Juli told her.

"Thanks." She fitted her key into the lock and the front door swung inward. The next moment, a blaze of light mingled with shouts of, "Surprise! Happy belated birthday, Shannon and Juli!"

Juli's jaw dropped even lower than Shannon's. "B-b-but—"

"You sound like a motorboat," Dave Gilmore teased. He took her jacket.

"This is supposed to be Shannon's party," she protested.

"My party?" Shannon turned and pointed an accusing finger. "You knew? How come I get a party now, even if it's for you, too?"

Juli threw her hands into the air. "All I know is that Amy asked me to help by getting you out of the way."

Shannon looked around the circle of smiling faces. "You're all sneaky, but I'm glad. I've never had a surprise party before." She sounded choked up. "Thanks, Amy. Everyone."

"From me too," Juli mumbled.

Amy danced over to them, light blue eyes shining at the

success of her plan. "If you're surprised now, just wait and see what's next. There's enough pizza in the kitchen to feed an army—or the boys—and something you'll never guess is coming afterwards."

Juli glanced at Shannon, who still looked as dumb-founded as Juli felt. How could they eat pizza on top of the big dinner Dad had fixed? Maybe they could pretend the excitement had affected their appetites. She asked her parents, "You knew all the time?"

"Of course." Anne Scott looked pleased with herself. "We can keep secrets. Now, what can I do to help, Amy?"

"Just cut the pizza. We cheated and had it delivered." The blond cheerleader giggled, obviously having fun. "We figured it was bad enough for the whole youth group to come barging in on Mr. Riley without messing up the kitchen making pizza."

Sean only laughed. "Next time, we'll do it from scratch."

"You can help them," Gary Scott told him. "You're probably better at handling the dough than anyone here."

"You can count on that," the banker retorted.

"Dad!" Juli and Shannon protested, but it was drowned out in a wave of silly puns that didn't subside until Amy asked Mr. Riley to give a blessing for the food.

The doorbell chimed just as the clock struck 9:30. "That must be her!" Amy was up and off like a startled robin. "She was supposed to be here an hour ago."

"Her? Who's 'her'?" Shannon whispered to Juli. "The

whole youth group is already here."

"I know." Again an unexplainable feeling of something not quite right gnawed at Juli. It exploded into disbelief when Amy came back with a stranger right behind her. Never outside of movies had Juli seen anyone dressed like the dark-skinned woman. How had Amy found a gypsy? Or was she an impersonator? Juli stifled a nervous giggle. Gypsy First Class was more like it. Real or otherwise, the woman with gold hoops in her ears was not a ragtag nobody. Her richly colored silk clothing was creaseless, as if the garments had just come from a high-class costume store.

"Meet Madame Zelda," Amy proudly announced. "I wanted something special. She's going to tell our fortunes."

The truth hit Juli with a sickening thud. This was why Amy had planned the party. Caught up in the coincidence of her horoscope reading coming just before news of her inheritance, now she planned to go a step farther. Juli looked at Sean and her parents' serious faces. If only they would do something. Anything!

Sean Riley cleared his throat. "We appreciate your kindness, Amy, but I really don't think—"

Juli tried to support him. "It's getting late and we have school tomorrow," she reminded. "The boys are in training. I'm sure Madame Zelda will understand, since she was late and everything." Juli hated herself for apologizing when she wanted to tell Amy only a jerk would bring a fake fortune teller to a church party! The look of misery on

Shannon's face stopped her. All the joy from having a surprise party had vanished when the gypsy, if she really were one, walked into the room.

The veiled but venomous look Juli received from the woman showed Madame Zelda did not appreciate Juli's interference. She shrugged shoulders covered by a glowing, heavily fringed shawl. "An accident on the freeway held me up," she explained in a deep voice. "You do not want to listen, so I will go." Her black gaze darted from face to face, came to rest on Shannon's. "It is too bad. Madame Zelda has much to say to this one."

*Get out. Get out and leave us alone!* Had Juli screamed the words? No, for the gypsy continued staring into Shannon's eyes, then turned on her heel and swept out. Juli felt as if an evil spirit had entered the peaceful Riley home and remained, even though Madame Zelda was no longer present.

Ted found his voice first. "What a bunch of garbage! Don't pay any attention to her mumbo jumbo, Shannon. Or would you call it mumble jumble?"

Amy turned on him. "It's not mumbo jumbo!" she cried. "Madame Zelda is a real gypsy. It cost me a lot of money just to convince her to come. I tried so hard to have a nice party and now it's ruined." She looked so much like a limp doll standing there with tears dripping, even Juli felt sorry for her.

Shannon ran to her and gave her a hug. "Most of it was wonderful, Amy." Her fierce glance at Juli and the others defied them to disagree. "It is a bit too late for Madame Zelda, especially when there's a gorgeous cake waiting to be cut, and didn't I see presents?"

Amy sniffled. "Y-yes."

"Stop crying, Amy," Ted gruffly told his sister. "If Shannon and Juli don't like their gifts, you can have them." His comment relaxed the tension.

When the girls opened twin boxes at the same time, Shannon cried, "No way does Amy get these!" Juli added, "Thanks, everyone." The group had gone together and purchased quality backpacks, perfect for school or hiking.

The rest of the party went smoothly, but a few chance, overheard words left Juli disturbed. When she came down from combing her hair in Shannon's room, her friend and Amy stood a little to one side. Juli heard Amy whisper, "Perhaps I can make a special appointment for you. Madame Zelda obviously has a message you really need to hear."

"I don't know." Shannon sounded doubtful.

"Look, I spent big bucks getting her here. The least you can do is listen to what she has to say." Amy glanced up at Juli and broke off before Shannon could reply.

On the way home Dad said, "I'm concerned about Amy getting into this fortune-telling business. You wouldn't believe how many teens and young adults are trapped in a web of deception by dabbling with horoscopes, Ouija boards, stuff like that. It's easy to believe that coincidences are actually the result of some random prediction." He sighed. "Too often they lead people into far more serious things, such as the occult."

"I just hope she doesn't pull Shannon in." Juli scuffed her tennis shoe on the sidewalk.

"You think that might happen?" Dad stopped and faced her. "Would you like for me to talk with your friend?"

"N-no." Juli didn't quite know how to explain. "Uh, Shannon likes you a lot, but she really doesn't know you all that well yet. Besides, she's a strong Christian. She'll be okay, won't she?"

"Unfortunately, we can't count too much on that," Dad warned. "Strong Christians, especially young people, are Satan's favorite targets. If he can tear them down, he knows it will influence a lot of others." He suddenly laughed. "We may be making too much of nothing. Shannon Riley appears to have her head on pretty straight."

"I hope so," Julie replied. But when she got home and ready for bed, she absentmindedly patted Clue, then wrote in her journal:

> *Am I making too big a deal out of tonight, God? I hope so. It's just that I don't want Shannon to get caught up in something evil. I don't want Amy to do that, either. What Dad said really scared me. Please, God, don't let Satan get hold of any more kids.*

Long after she turned out her light, Juli hugged Clue. So

what if she were sixteen now? Dr. Marlowe, the counselor who worked with her and Mom after Dad disappeared, was a lot older than that. She didn't have a Clue, but she had a floppy stuffed bunny instead. "It helps to hug him, and it's okay," she had told Juli.

"If Dr. Marlowe can do it, so can I. Right, Clue?" Her stuffed bear didn't answer, but his warm plush fur felt good against her cheek. Juli quickly said her prayers, resolved to tell Shannon exactly what Dad had said, and fell asleep.

She didn't get a chance in the morning. Shannon called and said her dad would give them a ride to school. Juli couldn't very well warn her about fortune-tellers and the occult in front of her dad. The only reference made to the night before was the banker's shrewd comment, "Amy tries too hard, doesn't she? Looks like you girls might be able to get in a little missionary work there." He chuckled. "Just don't let it turn out like the two parrots."

"Parrots?" Shannon said blankly.

"Haven't you heard the tale? It's been around for years. A minister who had a parrot felt sorry for another bird after his sailor owner died. He took the second parrot in, but was appalled to discover the bird used salty sea-language, not fit for the parsonage. The minister decided to put the birds in the same cage. His own parrot would set a good example by quoting bits of Scripture and hymns."

Juli had a sinking feeling in her stomach even before Sean added, "You can guess the rest of the story. Before long, the minister's parrot had picked up the other bird's bad language."

When neither of the girls laughed, the banker said, "It's only a story, but I'd hate to see you two take on Amy's ways."

Juli's heart felt strangely heavy. The second they got out of the car she turned to cry out that Shannon must not let Amy persuade her to keep the appointment for a private fortune-telling. She was too late. Before one word came out, Amy ran to them. "It's all set, Shannon. Today, right after school."

## CHAPTER 4

Shannon Riley stared out the side window of Amy Hilton's red Mustang convertible. Sheets of rain and gray skies matched her mood. *What am I doing here?* she asked herself. *Why did I let her talk me into this?* Feeling sorry for the chattering girl beside her didn't require that she go along with Amy when she insisted Shannon keep an appointment with the mysterious Madame Zelda, did it? Amy should never have hired a fortune-teller to show up at Juli's and Shannon's belated surprise birthday party.

Juli. Shannon's brain hit instant replay. She saw the disbelief in her best friend's blue eyes. She again heard anger in Juli's voice after Amy announced the date with Madame Zelda and fluttered away. "You're not going, are you?"

Her own troubled question, "What else can I do? Amy did spend a lot of money trying to give us a nice party." It sounded even weaker the second time around than it had when Juli confronted her.

"Look, Shannon. Dad says a lot of kids our age get hooked into some serious stuff that starts with fortunes and horoscopes."

"It's just for fun," Shannon had protested. "I'm not going to wind up being a crystal ball junkie or anything." She managed a small laugh.

"Unfunny. And how do you know?" Juli's piercing gaze bored into her. "I bet most of the other kids who first got involved felt the same way."

A feeling of hurt rose within Shannon. "Lighten up, will you? I'm going to listen to Madame Zelda to please Amy, then I'm out of there. It's that simple." She hesitated. "You wouldn't want to go with me, would you? You could wait outside with Amy." For a moment she thought Juli would say yes. Shannon hoped so. The more she thought about Madame Zelda, the less she liked the prospect of facing the fortune-teller's intense dark gaze that made her feel like a butterfly squirming on a pin.

"Thanks, but no thanks." Juli set her lips in a stubborn line, then marched off and didn't look back.

Shannon had felt terrible when Juli turned her back on her. Thinking about it now, she felt worse. Never in the course of their close friendship had she and Juli even come close to a serious quarrel. *Any quarrel,* her heart reminded, *except the disagreement over Amy's horoscope.* On the other hand, why did Juli think she knew everything? Just because her dad was a police officer didn't give her the right to run her friends' lives.

Shannon knew she was being unfair, but didn't care. Her Irish temper flared. Wouldn't a real friend have recognized how much Shannon needed her? How her heart had pounded so hard she wondered if everyone could hear it, when Madame Zelda said she had much to say to her? Where had Juli disappeared to for the rest of the day? She hadn't been in a single class they shared.

"Here we are." Amy swung into a parking place in front of a house set back from the street, across town from the Rileys' home.

"A private home? Doesn't she have a shop or something?" Shannon felt more uncomfortable than ever.

"It's here. See?" Amy pointed to a discreet sign near the front door that read: MADAME ZELDA.

"Amy, I really don't want to do this," Shannon said, desperately hoping to get out of the coming session.

The light blue eyes looked reproachful. "You promised."

"All right." Shannon sighed and opened the car door. Feeling like a roller coaster car that had no choice but to follow the one ahead, she followed Amy up the walk. What would it be like inside? Exotic tapestries? Bead curtains? Would Madame Zelda wear the same gypsy outfit she'd worn to the party?

To Shannon's surprise and relief, the dark woman came to the door wearing a flowing white silk·tunic and wide-legged pants. Only the gold hoop earrings and an intricate gold-thread pattern on the tunic collar relieved the stark white.

"Come in, children." She smiled, took them by the hand, and led them into a warm room, ordinary enough to fit most of the homes in Bellingham.

Shannon wanted to laugh. How did Amy like being called a child? A quick look showed she was more fascinated by Madame Zelda than ever. "Thank you for seeing Shannon privately," Amy said in a low voice.

"Think nothing of it. When one has the gift, one must use it." The fortune-teller turned to Shannon. "The moment I saw this one, I knew I must speak."

Her voice flowed like syrup on a hot pancake. It gave Shannon the creeps. "Uh, do you have a message for Amy, too?"

The dark eyes opened wide. "But of course. First, we must have refreshments, then Madame Zelda will share those things each of you needs to know." She clapped her hands sharply. A girl perhaps two years older than Shannon and Amy appeared with a tray. She walked as though she were in a trance.

*She looks like a zombie,* Shannon thought, repelled by the expressionless face.

The girl set the tray down, bowed, and exited as silently as she had come. Madame Zelda asked, "You like chocolate, don't you?"

"I do," Amy said.

Shannon just nodded. The liquid pouring into bone china cups from the silver pot smelled delicious, yet she felt reluctant to eat or drink in this house. *Don't be dumb,* she told herself. *Madame Zelda is probably a fake, but she's not going to poison us. You're getting as suspicious as Juli.* She grinned and relaxed, wishing Juli had come along to see how normal the fortune-teller was in her own home.

"This chocolate is wonderful!" Amy gushed after tasting it. "Do you have a special recipe?"

"It's Mexican chocolate, made with cinnamon. I'm glad you like it."

Shannon had to admit she'd never tasted better chocolate. Its warmth spread through her. She also liked the small, flaky, honey pastries served with the whipped-cream-topped chocolate.

When they finished, Madame Zelda said, "I will speak to the little one first." She rose and smiled. "Come, please." She hesitated, then told Shannon, "You, my child, must relax. You need not fear what I have to tell you. Would you like more hot chocolate?"

"Please." Shannon felt herself blush. How transparent she must be! Guilt filled her for fearing their hostess. Madame Zelda had chatted with them while they ate, acting genuinely interested in the girls' friends and school activities. "I am a little nervous," Shannon confessed. "I've never had my fortune told before."

Madame Zelda's long, white fingers tilted the silver

chocolate pot over Shannon's cup. "That is strange, since you come from Ireland." She laughed merrily. It made her seem less glamorous, more of a real person. "Ireland is a land of charms and enchantment, with its leprechauns and misty dells. No matter. Finish your chocolate and I will be ready for you soon."

Amy obediently followed the woman out of the room. Shannon heard the soft sound of their footsteps, muffled by thick carpet, then the opening and closing of a door. She sipped her chocolate, helped herself to another pastry, and waited, more curious now than apprehensive.

The combination of the warm room and chocolate made Shannon drowsy. She yawned and hoped Amy wouldn't take too long. It would be so embarrassing to yawn in the fortune-teller's face. She giggled at the thought and yawned again.

Amy burst back into the room, ecstatic as the day she learned about her inheritance. "Shannon, it's great! Wait 'til you hear what she told me—"

"Child, child," Madame Zelda interrupted. "Do not fill your friend's head with your fortune. She must think clearly in order to receive her own. Come."

Shannon followed the woman down a long hall and into a small room. She blinked to adjust her eyes to the dim light, noticing the lack of furniture. Two straight chairs stood beside a small table in the middle of the room. The pleasant fragrance of blended spices filled the air. A black, velvet-shrouded mound in the center of the table was the only other object in the room.

Shannon hesitated just inside the doorway. A tiny warning bell rang in her brain. The next moment, Madame Zelda laid a comforting hand on her arm. "There really is nothing to fear." She led Shannon to a chair, seated herself across from her, and removed the velvet. A shining crystal ball about the size of a soccer ball appeared.

Shannon gazed at it, marveling at the rainbows of color reflected in its depths, that soon changed to swirling, murky white.

"Is something wrong, child?"

"The crystal ball. I—I don't feel comfortable," Shannon stammered.

"Very well." Madame Zelda sounded amused. She covered the ball, removed it from the table, and carried it out of the room. When she returned, she quietly said, "I have no need of the ball. It is only a prop, a point of concentration especially good at parties and for those like your friend Amy." She smiled and her face looked kinder than Shannon had seen it so far.

Relieved, Shannon leaned forward. Why did she feel she stood on the edge of a great mystery? As she had told Juli, this was only for fun.

Madame Zelda softly quoted, " 'Now faith is the substance of things hoped for, the evidence of things not seen.' Have faith, child," she said. "Faith can unlock the key to all you hope for, and give you evidence of those things you cannot see. Are there not things you wish to know, things you can ask no one?"

A quiver ran through Shannon. She thought of how hard she and her father had struggled to make a new life after her mother died. She remembered her fears when Father said they were moving to America. Even after finding Juli and making friends, deep inside lay an ever-present fear. What if something so terrible happened that it robbed her of that friendship, the way death had stolen her mother? Shannon whispered, "Oh, yes! I—"

"You need not tell me. I already know." The fortune-teller's soothing voice lowered. "You have come a long way, child, from a land far from here. There you knew much happiness, but also much sorrow." She went on to tell Shannon incidents from her childhood and youth before she said, "This has left you with fear, the fear others you love will be taken from you as well.

"I cannot promise this will not come to pass. Yet, know this. There will be those sent into your life whose love and friendship will wrap you in a blanket of protection. You will find great joy in their presence. You will discover a life so much above anything you have ever known, many times you shall marvel." Shannon tried to memorize every word she'd said during the long silence that followed. If Juli were here, her doubts would flee. Madame Zelda was no fake, but a person permitted to see into the lives of others and bring them great comfort.

"Trust me, child." She sounded sad. "Many choose not to believe, so to them cannot be given. Do not the Scriptures tell us, in Luke 11:9, to ask, that we might receive? To seek, that we might find? To knock, that the door might be opened? Should some doubt, still you can know these things are true." Again she fell silent. "Child, are there questions you wish to ask?"

Shannon shook her head.

"It is enough for today," Madame Zelda said. She rose, came around the table and laid her hand on the dark, bowed head. "You must come again, child, and learn more of what I can tell you. It will be given a little at a time, as you are ready and able to accept it."

"Why?" Shannon burst out. "When you have this gift, and quote Scripture and everything, why do you cheapen it by hiring yourself out as a gypsy?"

The hand on her hair pressed down ever so lightly. "I work as I am permitted," Madame Zelda said. "I say pleasant things to Amy and others like her; not lies, but possibilities. In the meantime, I seek those rare persons into whose lives I am given insight. Only to them will be known the mysteries of the universe. You are one of the special ones, Shannon Riley, one of those chosen to learn far more than most who inhabit this planet. When will you come again?"

"I'm not sure," she whispered. "May I call you?"

"Certainly, but do not wait too long. I am unable to tell how much time I will be given in which to instruct you before I must move on to someone who needs me even more." She stepped back and silently escorted the dazed girl back to where Amy waited.

"Wasn't it wonderful? Aren't you glad I made you come?" Amy demanded when they got in the Mustang and headed for home.

Shannon stared out the window into the rainy early evening. "I don't know." Away from the warm room and Madame Zelda's compelling gaze, some of the woman's charisma lessened. The whole experience felt more dream than real.

"What did she tell you?"

Shannon didn't want to discuss it with Amy. "Stuff about my parents. How about you?"

Amy chattered all the way home about how popular Madame Zelda had said she was, how fortunate to be a cheerleader, and have her own car.

*Nothing I couldn't have found out with a bit of research,* Shannon realized. Yet it didn't explain some of the things Madame Zelda knew about the Rileys. The question in Shannon's mind, however, was what Juli would say. She couldn't wait to see her friend, even though Juli had walked out on her. "Drop me at the Scotts, will you, please?"

"Maybe Juli will go with us next time. You *are* going again, aren't you?"

For the second time, Shannon replied, "I don't know. See you tomorrow." She watched the red Mustang drive out of sight before slowly going up the walk. Rain continued to fall.

"Give me your coat, second daughter," Anne Scott ordered when the wet girl stepped into the hall. "Juli's studying in her room." Her warm smile showed Juli hadn't said anything about the argument.

"Thanks." Shannon started down the hall to the bedroom as familiar as her own. For the first time, she felt reluctant to see Juli. *"This has left you with the fear others you love will be taken from you,"* Madame Zelda had said. What if she were right? What if the friendship that changed a scared fifteen-year-old Irish immigrant's life weakened and died? She swallowed hard. All the promises in the world that others would love and comfort her didn't help.

Bowing her head, Shannon desperately prayed, "Please, God. Don't let it happen!" She raised her hand and fearfully knocked on the closed bedroom door.

# CHAPTER 5

When Juli marched away from Shannon and didn't look back, her numb feet carried her up the school steps, straight into Dave Gilmore! He dropped his books and caught her by the elbows to keep her from falling. "What's the rush?" he teased. Then, "Juli, what's wrong?"

The concern in his voice and fear over what Shannon might be walking into brought a spurt of tears behind Juli's eyelids. She held her eyes wide open to keep the tears from falling. "I had a fight with Shannon."

"You *what?*" He dropped his hands, blue eyes shocked. "I don't believe it!"

"Believe it." Misery spilled out. "She's going with Amy to get her fortune told by that designer gypsy. Dad says a lot of kids who mess with stuff like fortunes get involved in really heavy stuff later."

"Why is she doing something like that?" Dave demanded, hands on his hips. "She's one of the strongest Christians in our group."

"I know, but Amy convinced her it was her duty." Juli grimaced. "She said the least Shannon could do was go, after Amy spent all that money."

"Just the kind of appeal that would get to Shannon," Dave muttered. Some of the concern left his face. "I wouldn't worry too much about it. She'll come back laughing, and that will be the end of it."

"That's exactly what she said. She asked me to go with her and wait outside." Juli bent and picked up Dave's books to prevent him from seeing how miserable she felt.

"I suppose you told her no way."

"Of course! What else could I do?" She straightened and glared at him.

"I'm not putting you down," Dave protested. He half closed his eyes and crossed his arms over his navy sweater. "How did she sound when she asked?"

Juli tried to remember. "I was really mad—"

"Angry. Dogs go mad," he corrected.

She recognized it as an attempt to cheer her up. "Okay, angry." Juli thought some more. How had she missed seeing the wistful expression in Shannon's eyes? Or hearing the appeal in her voice? A sickening conclusion made her feel hollow in spite of a big breakfast. "I should have gone," she cried. "Shannon's been there for me every time I needed her. The one time she reached out to me, I let her down!" Juli felt blood drain from her face. "What am I going to do?"

"I'm no counselor, but knowing you two, I'd say all you have to do is tell her you're sorry," Dave suggested. "Come on, I'll walk you to your first class. Is Shannon in it?"

"Not this quarter." She lengthened her stride to keep up with his long legs. "I'll have to see her later."

"Good luck. Uh-oh. There's the bell." He gave Juli an encouraging grin before they reached the principal's office, and he loped off down the hall.

"I have the feeling I'm going to need it," she muttered. Swimming in a sea of regret, the second bell caught her before she got to her classroom. Great. Now she had to get a slip from the office for being tardy. What a rotten day!

It got worse. Juli no sooner entered the office than the secretary said, "Talk about perfect timing! I was just going to send someone for you. Your mother said to have you call this number."

"She did? I don't recognize it." Juli quickly dialed. "Mom? What's wrong?"

"He's all right now, but Dad had to come to Emergency." Anne Scott gave the name of a local hospital. "Take a taxi. If you don't have enough money, I'll meet you at the door. Remember: Dad's okay. I just need you here with me."

The longest twenty minutes of Juli's life stretched between the time she hung up and when she flew into her mother's arms. "What happened?"

"Dad felt dizzy and light-headed just after we left. He called 9-1-1, then my school. An ambulance brought him in." Mom's lips trembled. "I've been afraid something like this might happen. The shooting plus the stress of the last year has put a terrible strain on him. The doctors don't think it's his heart, but they'll be running tests."

Juli felt her world was falling apart. "It isn't fair," she whispered. "Just when he gets home and is getting over being shot, this happens."

"It's probably just a warning signal," her mother comforted.

"If it's Dad's heart, he's out of police work, except for maybe office jobs. Right?"

Mom just looked at her.

"At least he'd be safe from criminals." The words Juli had held back ever since Dad came home popped out unexpectedly.

"I don't believe exchanging that kind of danger for a bad heart is a fair trade," Mom said sharply. She relented when Juli hung her head. "I know you didn't mean it, Juli. You're just worried. So am I."

Several hours later, the Scotts' family physician, Dr. Marlowe, who had been in consultation with hospital personnel, came out smiling. Juli's spirits rose immediately and her mother's face brightened. "Nothing wrong with Gary Scott except delayed stress," Dr. Marlowe told them. "His nerves have taken a tremendous beating. Now he simply needs to rest and build up his strength. No more talk of going back to work for at least another couple of months." She laughed. "I can't promise you two will live through it, but he certainly will!" The doctor sobered. "It would be good for him to come up with an absorbing interest. What does he enjoy most?"

"Being outdoors, church, and detective magazines," Juli promptly told her. "He reads them all the time. You know, the kind where you try to figure out the ending by catching all the subtle clues." She grinned. "Dad is so good at solving the mysteries, Mom says he should be writing them." Excitement beat in her brain, then faded. "I suppose writing that kind of story would be too stressful?"

Dr. Marlowe looked thoughtful. "Perhaps not," she slowly said. "Sounds to me like a lot of it is logistical. Church is great. So is the outdoors stuff as long as he doesn't overdo. The same for writing, if he wants to give it a try."

"I just might give writing a try," Dad said after the hospital released him and they arrived home. He laughed. "Sure you can stand the competition, Juli?"

"Yeah. Besides, if you get good enough, I might consider letting you collaborate with me!" She giggled.

"All right, you two, no funny stuff," Anne sternly told them. "Remember, Gary, Dr. Marlowe says no more than two hours a day writing, and she wants to check your progress weekly."

"Yes, ma'am," he grumbled, even though his lips

twitched. "I can see I'm going to be as pampered around here as Clue. Hey, maybe I need a mascot, too. How does *Murder in Black and White,* alias *The Case of the Stuffed Skunk* sound?"

"It stinks!" Juli laughed until she cried. Neither Mom's shocked, "Juli!" nor Dad's haughty stare could stop her. When she finally got in control again, she felt better than she had since she called Mom and raced to the hospital.

Gary Scott had the last laugh. He raised one eyebrow and announced, "Just for that I *will* write the story." A gleam came into his gray eyes. "I can always submit it under a pseudonym. *Juli Scott* would make a great pen name, right?"

"You wouldn't!"

He smirked. "I know that, but how can you be so sure?"

"Anyone who acts the way you are now can't have much wrong with them," Mom commented. Dad only laughed again and winked at Juli, but she noticed how little protest he made when Mom shooed him off to take a nap.

"It's like once Dr. Marlowe ordered him to stay home, he stopped fighting it," Juli whispered to Mom in the kitchen. "I'm so glad he's going to be all right."

"So am I." Anne Scott looked at the clock. "You've missed all but your last class. There isn't much point in your going back to school now, is there?"

"Not really," Juli replied, wanting to shout she had every reason to get back to school, especially before Shannon took off with Amy. Mom's expression stopped her. She obviously could use some moral support after the trying day. An apology to Shannon would have to wait. "I'll put my books in my room and be right back," Juli promised. She headed down the hall.

How long would Shannon and Amy stay with Madame What's-her-face? An hour? Two? Where did the woman live, anyway? She had chalked up being late to an accident on the freeway. Which freeway? Was she actually in Bellingham, or had she slithered in from somewhere else?

"Now if this were a fairy tale, she'd appear in a puff of magician's smoke," Juli told Clue while trying to figure out the best time to call Shannon. "Too bad we can't make her disappear the same way!" She padded barefoot to the kitchen and the sound of Mom beating something in a bowl. "Mmm. Chocolate cake?"

"Brownies. As long as I'm here early, I thought I'd play homemaker."

Juli parked on a kitchen stool. "You really miss it, don't you?"

"Yes, but I also enjoy teaching." Mom sighed. A wistful look crept into the blue eyes so like her daughter's. "That's one of the things we have to talk about before the end of the year." She stopped stirring and poured the rich chocolate batter into a pan. "It doesn't seem likely Gary will be off the force for an extended period of time. But if he is, we will need the money." She smiled and lifted her chin in the air. "I'm just the gal who can earn it."

"Right." Juli slid from the stool and hugged her. "You're the best, Mom. Even if the word 'gal' is hopelessly out of date, you aren't!" She grabbed the phone directory. "What was that fortune-teller's name, the one Amy hired?"

Mom looked surprised at the sudden change of subject. "Madame Zell?. . . No, Zelda. Why?"

"Just curious to see which rock Amy found her under. Sorry," Juli added when Mom gave her a disapproving look. "That wasn't nice, was it?"

"No. I didn't care for the woman either, but God loves her just as much as He loves us."

Juli ran a finger down the Z's in the phone book. "I know. Oh, here she is: *Zelda, Madame*. Isn't it funny that she's listed under her first name." She checked the address. "Good. She's about as far across town from us as she can get." She snapped the directory shut. "Need some help?"

"Not until time to set the table. If you have homework, this is a good time to do it. Shannon's sure to drop by later. She'll want to hear about your day."

"Not as much as I want to hear about hers," Juli muttered to herself when she got out of listening range. She went back to her bedroom but instead of tackling her homework, she curled up on her bed. How could she concentrate after a day like this? The look on her best friend's face when Juli walked away haunted her. Even before Shannon could be expected to get home, Juli punched in her number. The phone rang four times, then the answering machine clicked on. Juli hung up. A half hour later, she tried again. And a half hour after that. Both times she got the answering machine, but didn't leave a message. How could she say "I'm sorry" when Sean Riley might be the one to get the message? It would mean explanations neither she nor Shannon cared to make.

"Time to set the table, Juli." Mom's cheerful voice and Dad's low rumble forced her to abandon attempts to reach Shannon. Yet all through Mom's creamy chicken casserole and crisp tossed salad followed by brownies, Juli waited for the phone to ring. Unwilling to involve her parents, Juli impatiently loaded the dishwasher and excused herself. Shannon must be home by now. Was she so upset by what happened this morning that she wouldn't call?

Juli slipped into the den and tried again.

"Riley residence," Sean's deep voice said.

Juli quickly hung up, feeling guilty but unwilling to talk with him. If Shannon hadn't come home, he would be sure to think she was at Juli's. If only she were! Juli dragged back to her room, closed the door so she wouldn't be disturbed, and knelt by her bed. "Lord, I've made a mess of things. Will You please help?" After a long time, she got up and lay back down on her bed, hugging Clue and waiting a reasonable length of time before trying to call Shannon.

A few minutes that felt like hours later, she heard a soft tap-tap on her door.

"Who is it?" Juli sat up, Clue still in her arms.

"Shannon."

Happiness poured through her. She bounded off the bed and across the room, dangling Clue from one hand. She jerked open the door, grabbed her friend's arm, and pulled her inside. "I am so glad you're here!" Even in her elation, she noticed the hesitant look in Shannon's blue-gray eyes. A pang went through her.

Laughter replaced the strained expression. "Mercy me, you're for bein' excited!" Juli almost came unglued with relief. Wherever she had been, whatever she had seen, heard, or done, the old Shannon freed her arm and sat down on the extra twin bed. Juli put Clue on the desk and parked on her own bed.

"How come you cut classes? You did, didn't you? Was it because I made you mad?" Some of Shannon's hesitancy returned.

"Dogs go mad, people get angry," Juli told her.

Shannon rolled her eyes. "Answer my question, Juli Scott, before I do something awful to you." Her wide smile weakened the threat.

"He's okay now, but Dad had to go to the hospital. Mom called me to be with her." Juli hurriedly sketched in all that had happened. When Shannon looked alarmed, she added, "He's fine now. Really. He just has to give himself time to heal."

"I'm sorry," Shannon whispered. "I didn't even know there was a problem." A crystal drop slipped down her cheek and plopped onto her hand.

"*You're* sorry! I'm the one who's sorry. You really wanted me to go with you today, didn't you?"

Shannon glanced down and looked unhappy. "Yes, but it's okay."

"It's not okay. Friends should be there when you need them," Juli said fiercely. She jumped up, hugged Shannon, and settled back down on her own bed. "So what happened? With Madame Zelda, I mean?"

"I don't know."

Disappointment fell on Juli like March rain. She'd hoped Shannon would come back laughing and the whole thing would be over. "What do you mean?"

Shannon looked troubled. "She isn't at all like she was at my house. She told me I was special and would know great happiness. She seems totally sincere. She also uses Scripture, Juli. Verses about having faith, asking and receiving."

The more the Irish girl talked, the worse Juli felt. She could almost see strong, invisible chains starting to tighten around her friend.

# CHAPTER 6

It was all Juli could do to keep from crying out in protest when Shannon repeated what Madame Zelda had told her. She mentally ordered herself to stop, and to listen. Shannon obviously at least half believed in the fortune-teller. Coming down on her like an avalanche could make things even worse.

*If it were the other way around, what could Shannon say to help without antagonizing me?* Juli wondered. A silent prayer for help went up from her heart. She waited. No bolt of lightning followed. No crack of thunder, or a light from heaven. Just a feeling she needed to be as understanding as possible.

Shannon finished and sat looking at Juli with troubled eyes. "Well?"

Juli played for time. "Do you know what she told Amy?"

"Nothing she couldn't be expected to know with a little research," Shannon admitted. "That's what bothers me. Anyone could find out Amy's a cheerleader who drives a red Mustang convertible she got from inherited money." She giggled and little crinkles came at the corners of her eyes. "The way Amy's been blowing her own trumpet, most of Bellingham knows!"

Juli didn't bother to tell her it was 'blowing her own horn,' not trumpet.

"I just don't understand how Madame Zelda could know some of the things she told me, especially about my childhood in Ireland," Shannon said. "I don't want to believe her, but when I was there, I had a strange feeling I was on the edge of discovering answers to a mystery." Her long, dark lashes covered her eyes.

*Great. Now what?* Juli glanced around the room, scrambling for an idea. Her gaze stopped at her homework. A little thrill went through her. "Sometimes when I'm trying to decide something, it helps to make a list of opposites. You know, goods and not-so-goods." She felt like she was blathering, the word Shannon used for people who talked on and on without making sense. To her amazement, Shannon perked right up.

"Good idea. Why don't you write?"

"Okay." Juli grabbed a notebook and pencil.

Shannon frowned and looked unhappy. She fidgeted with her fingers and when she spoke, her voice sounded small. "There's a problem. I don't know what's good and what's not-so-good."

"Why don't we just write everything down chrono-logically and decide later?" Juli suggested, pencil poised and ready.

"All right. First, Amy bored me to death on the way there." Some of Shannon's gloom lifted. "That's definitely a not-so-good."

Juli began writing. "I'll mark the ones we know as G or NSG. Next?"

"I told Amy I really didn't want to see Madame Zelda. That's good, maybe?"

"Sure. Keep talking."

"I felt really weird when we rang the doorbell." Shannon closed her eyes. "I guess because I didn't know what to expect." Her eyes popped open. "NSG?"

"Uh-huh. How did you feel when you got inside?"

"A little weird, but relieved. The house is ordinary and Madame Zelda was dressed right for going out to dinner at a nice restaurant." Shannon laughed and sounded more like herself. "The refreshments get a Y for yummy. I never tasted anything better than the honey pastry and Mexican chocolate made with cinnamon and whipped cream."

Juli's pencil paused. She forced herself to say casually, "Sounds terrific. We'll have to try it that way sometime. Did you have seconds?"

Shannon nodded. A small smile crept to her lips. "Two cups of chocolate and three or four honey pastries. Amy just had one cup because she went first. The weird thing is, by the time she came back I thought I was going to yawn in Madame Zelda's face. The refreshments and warm room made me drowsy."

An alarm went off in Juli's brain. Had the chocolate been drugged? Again she bit her tongue to keep from blurting out her suspicions. "Were you still nervous when she came back with Amy?"

Shannon shook her head. "No. I did feel funny when I saw the crystal ball on the table. When I told Madame Zelda that, she took it away. She only uses it for show, with people like Amy, she said."

Juli frantically scribbled while Shannon repeated the rest of the fortune, then moved to one side of her bed. "Come over here and we'll go over the list."

"Okay." Shannon came to sit beside her. Golden-brown and dark heads bent over the good and not-so-good list. Some items didn't have a G or NSG, and both girls admitted they weren't sure how to mark them. After they went through the introductory part, they came to the actual fortune. Juli had numbered the points.

1. *Madame Zelda quoted Scripture.*
2. *Shannon had come a long way, from a far land.*
3. *Shannon had known much happiness, but also much sorrow.*
4. *This left her with the fear of losing others she loved.*

5.  *Madame Zelda couldn't promise it wouldn't happen.*
6.  *If it did, other people would bring Shannon joy, protection, a better life.*
7.  *Shannon was to trust her, rather than those who didn't believe.*
8.  *More would be given, a little at a time, as Shannon was able to accept it.*
9.  *Madame Zelda felt Shannon was one of the special "chosen ones," into whose life she had been given insight.*
10. *Shannon must come again soon, before Madame Zelda moved on to someone who needs her more.*

Juli stared at the list. Writing down the fortune made it even more ominous, simply because it sounded so believable! She struggled to hide her real feelings and said, "Let's take them point by point. It's good that Madame Zelda quotes Scripture. On the other hand, anyone who knows the Bible or has a concordance can find verses to prove a point."

"True," Shannon admitted. "Items 5 through 7 are also pretty general."

"Numbers 8 through 10 could be to hook you into coming back," Juli put in.

Shannon's eyes looked enormous, more gray than blue, when she glanced up. "I just don't understand how she could know 2, 3, and especially 4."

"Even though you've lost a lot of your Irish accent, it's still pretty plain you weren't born in America," Juli slowly said. Excitement rose within her. "And Amy could have told Madame Zelda your mother died."

Shannon's shoulders slumped. "So we've accounted for everything but number 4. Juli, I never told anyone, not even you, how afraid I am something might happen to Dad, or Grand, or you." Tears glittered and she impatiently brushed them away. "How could Madame Zelda know?"

Again Julie sent up a silent prayer for help. After a minute she said, "It kind of goes with losing someone you love." A lump swelled in her throat. "All the time Dad was gone I kept wondering what I'd do if anything happened to Mom."

"Really?" Shannon sat up straight. Her face brightened. "Then Madame Zelda didn't actually know as much about me as she pretended." She jumped off the bed. "Yes! I can forget her and her fortunes." She whirled, hugged Juli, and grinned. "I bet Amy won't forget hers. She heard everything she wanted to hear. I guess that's why people go to fortune-tellers. Right?"

Juli nodded, but the whisper of a doubt remained. "Uh, you aren't going back again, are you?"

Shannon looked surprised and sat back down on the other twin bed. "After we figured out an explanation for everything she told me? Why should I? I do feel kind of sorry for her. She sounded so sincere. Sad, too, that more people didn't believe in her. Maybe she really thinks she has some kind of gift and can see into people's lives."

The whisper grew louder and drummed in Juli's ears. Was there still a bond, even though weakened, between Shannon and Madame Zelda? She sighed. "Only God can do that."

Shannon ended the serious discussion by saying, "I'm not so sure. You're no fortune-teller, but most of the time you know what I'm thinking!"

"Right, so you'd better watch it." The strong feeling she should say something else caused Juli to add, "I wonder if Madame Zelda informs herself as well about all her clients as she obviously did about you and Amy." Juli kept her voice calm. "Remember, your dad's a banker."

"So what?" Shannon looked astonished.

"So don't you watch TV or read the newspapers? There are a lot of crazies out there who might think getting hold of you could bring them big bucks."

Shannon burst out laughing. "Sounds like a headline: *Mysterious Figures Abduct Local Banker's Daughter.*" Her eyes twinkled. "Local banker's daughter has homework waiting and had better go. Is someone walking me home or shall I call Dad?"

Gary Scott said he was too tired for a walk in the rain, but Mom and Juli put on shiny rain slickers and went with Shannon, who proudly announced, "I'm getting my car this weekend. A blue Honda Accord, just a couple of years old."

"Really? Will you be driving it to school?" Juli asked.

"Sometimes." Shannon made a face. "With the price of gas, I'd use up my allowance practically before Dad gave it to me. I'll probably just drive when we have to stay after school for something special."

"Great."

Juli felt wonderful. Dad was home and going to be all right. Shannon had more important things to worry about than fortune-tellers. "God's in His heaven—all's right with the world," she quoted to Mom on the way home.

"Robert Browning in Pippa Passes," Anne Scott said. "You're certainly in a good mood." She laughed. "So am I. I'd been hoping Dr. Marlowe would ground Gary for a longer time." She tipped her head back and let the rain that had dwindled to mist settle on it. Light from the street lamps lent a sheen to her face.

Juli gave her a quick hug, glad for their time together. How many times had they walked Shannon home since last fall? First, through falling, golden leaves. Next, on whitened sidewalks with frosty air or gentle flakes swirling around them. Now, with spring coming on. She quoted the rest of the passage Mrs. Sorenson had taught her to love:

"The year's at the spring and day's at the morn;
Morning's at seven; the hill-side's dew-pearled;
The lark's on the wing: the snail's on the thorn—"

Mom's voice chimed in, "God's in His heaven—all's right with the world."

Laughing together, they reached home with its bright

windows that welcomed them and fought back the falling night shadows.

Juli's carefree mood lasted all through the bus ride to school with Shannon and her morning classes. Amy shattered it at lunch with a play-by-play account of her trip to Madame Zelda with Shannon.

"You actually dragged her there?" Ted asked his sister.

Amy pouted. "She went willingly enough."

Juli rolled her eyes and Dave Gilmore grunted. Shannon said nothing. The lukewarm reaction didn't even slow Amy down. She tossed her head and repeated what she'd told Shannon on the way home. She defiantly told the others they should go see the fortune-teller and find out what she knew about them. "I'll be glad to take you," she offered, with a sweeping glance of lashes at Dave.

Shannon giggled and poked Juli with her elbow, but Juli caught Dave's grin from across the table and went from disgusted to merely annoyed. So what if Amy made a big deal out of it? She did the same with everything that happened. Why let it ruin the day? Juli held onto the thought and managed to feel upbeat until honors writing, the last class of the day.

"Juli and Shannon, please stay for a few minutes," Mrs. Sorensen said just before the bell rang. When the room cleared she smiled at the girls. "Are both of you entering the magazine contest?"

"I am, but I don't know what I'm going to write yet,"

Juli confessed.

"I'm still thinking about it." A mischievous look came into Shannon's expressive face. "Mrs. Sorenson, could I enter the story 'Katie' that I wrote for class fall quarter?"

"Just what I intended to suggest," the teacher quickly agreed. "You'll want to polish it some more, of course, using what you've learned since then." She paused. "I won't be at all surprised if it at least places."

Juli's heart sank. What chance did she have against "Katie"? She remembered the day Shannon read her story of a fictional teenage girl who lived through the Irish potato famine. In the simplest of words, she took the class inside Katie's heart and mind. She showed the hunger and death, and the miserable ships called *coffin boats*, in which those who escaped sickness and starvation came to America. Juli didn't think she'd ever forget the end of the story. Katie hugged a younger sister and said, "Don't fret, darlin'. Tomorrow will be for bringin' us better things." The class had reacted with silence, followed by a storm of cheers.

How proud she had been of her friend. How insignificant her own story, even though it had seemed *Seventeen*-quality when she wrote it! *I'll have to do better than that to beat her,* Juli thought. Yet so far she just didn't know what to write.

An idea flicked into her mind, too elusive to hold. She tried to capture it without success. Yet all the way home on the bus, it ran beneath her conversation with Shannon like the undertow in the Skagit River. After supper and dishes she asked, "Anyone using the computer tonight?"

" 'Not I, said the little red hen,' " Mom quoted. "Guess what story I read to my first-graders today?"

"Not I." Dad yawned and looked smug. "I put in my two hours this morning."

"You did?" Juli felt her smile widen. "What did you write?"

Her father's nose went into the air. "Smart writers don't give away their ideas. Remember, work on paper is automatically copyrighted. Ideas can't be."

"I won't steal your ideas," Juli sputtered. Dad would be disappointed if she didn't try, though, she knew.

"Let's not say steal. Borrow, maybe?" His gray eyes sparkled. "You know what? Even if I never sell anything, that was two of the most enjoyable hours I've spent in a long time." He relented enough to add, "I didn't start a story. I just brainstormed a possible plot, starting with the end and working backwards."

"That is really cool," Juli told him. "Thanks for the help."

"Help? What help?" Dad asked suspiciously. His only answer was a maddening grin and a trill of laughter when Juli raced down the hall to the den before she lost the stupendous idea knocking at the door of her brain.

# CHAPTER 7

*Tap. Tap-tap-tap.* Juli's fingers flew over the computer keyboard. Her cheeks burned and her thoughts ran even faster than her fingers. Dad's comment about writing down the end of the story first and working backwards had unleashed a torrent of ideas. If only the rest of the story would go as well as the outline!

At last Juli leaned back, scrolled through the text, and read what she had written. A big grin spread over her face. The random notes on the screen practically stood up and shouted the possibility of her best story so far. She printed them, then saved her work on a floppy disk and labeled it JULI.

Back in her bedroom, Juli read her ideas aloud in a low voice. Mrs. Sorenson said it was the best way to catch errors and get the feel for a story. "Ears catch what eyes miss, especially in your own work," the teacher often warned. "It also helps when choosing a title."

Juli remembered more of Mrs. Sorenson's advice: "Figure out the theme, the underlying message that supports your whole manuscript. Write it in one sentence and post it near your computer. You may never use it in the story, but doing this helps keep you on track." Most of her students found the simple exercise difficult, but it worked.

"So what's my theme?" Juli thought of her basic plot idea—a family who decorates their home for Christmas but holds bitterness in their hearts toward one another. "I know," she murmured to Clue, who continued to stare at her with his shiny black eyes. "It takes more than tinsel to make a happy Christmas. I can use it for a title, too: 'More Than Tinsel.' Yes!" She wrote it at the top of her page, dropped her pen, and hugged the plushy brown bear.

Now to let the story simmer like homemade soup, so the flavors would blend and her subconscious could work on it while she did other things. For the next few days, bits and pieces came at odd times. In the middle of a test. Just before she fell asleep. While she was talking with friends. Juli faithfully jotted them down, and dropped them in a Christmasy-red file folder conspicuously marked "More Than Tinsel." She would know when they were ready to be written.

Mrs. Sorenson was giving anyone who entered the magazine contest credit for their stories. Juli worked hard on the required mini-outline. She finally came up with what the teacher called a "dust jacket blurb," the short synopsis used inside book covers or on the back of the book to attract readers. Mrs. Sorenson's eyes sparkled when she read:

> *Sixteen-year-old Wendy Thompson spends hours decorating her home for Christmas. Yet all the holly wreaths and candles, bright lights and presents can't erase bitter memories or the anger between her brother and her parents.*
>
> *Wendy knows it will take more than tinsel to bring peace and joy to the Thompson home this holiday season. How can she bring the real meaning of Christmas into a house where no one else seems to care?*

"Good, Juli!" the teacher exclaimed. "There's room here for a lot of honest sentiment. Don't let it get sticky, but don't be afraid to climb inside Wendy and write about the way she feels."

Shannon was even more complimentary when she read it. " 'More than Tinsel' is not only good, it's going to be great. So much for my poor 'Katie'! She doesn't have a chance," she complained when they walked down the hall to their lockers. Her heartwarming smile made Juli feel good all over, but Juli only said, "Don't be silly. It will take a lot of good writing to make Wendy that appealing. You're so lucky. You already have 'Katie' almost finished.

I'm just getting started on my story." She anxiously looked at her friend. "To do a good job, I'm going to have to concentrate. We won't get to be together as much for the next couple of weeks."

"I know." A shadow blotted out Shannon's happiness. "It's too bad it came right now, when—"

"Wait up, will you?" Dave Gilmore loped down the hall toward them. "I hear you got your car, Shannon. How do you like it?"

"Fine." Her sparkle returned. "It may not be a red Mustang convertible, but it's mine, all mine."

Juli felt guilty. She'd been so absorbed in her story, she'd barely congratulated Shannon on her purchase. *We haven't really been out in it,* she defended herself. *Just last night for a short ride.* Eager to make amends, she quickly said, "It's wonderful, and the prettiest shade of blue."

"Thanks." Shannon grinned at her. "Let's plan on doing something Saturday morning, okay?"

Juli regretfully shook her head. "I can't. Some friends of Dad and Mom's are coming for an early dinner and I have to help get ready."

"Another time, then." Shannon's careless answer didn't hide her disappointment.

"I'll be happy to go somewhere with you," Amy Hilton's high-pitched voice sang out from behind them.

"So will I," her mischievous twin added. "Come on. We'll walk you to class and talk about it."

Shannon glanced at Juli, shrugged, and walked away

between them. Juli felt like a pup in a pet store whose littermates had all been sold.

"Amy's sure been trying to hang out with Shannon lately," Dave observed. His blue eyes darkened. "Do you know if she's gone back to that fortune-teller?"

"I don't think Shannon did, and since Amy hasn't said anything, I guess she hasn't, either." Juli took the books she needed from her locker and matched her steps to Dave's longer ones.

"If she went I'm sure we'd have heard," Dave agreed. "See you later." He left her at the door to her next class and hurried off down the hall.

Juli watched him go. He was so cool. Understanding, too. Incredible how his grin always lifted her spirits. She might be his girlfriend *pro tem*, as he'd said, but she never felt pressured, just glad he'd chosen her.

The Saturday dinner went fine. After the visitors left, Juli called Shannon to see how she had spent the day. She got the answering machine. She tried a couple of times later, with no luck. Why should it bother her? Obviously Sean Riley had taken his daughter somewhere. The Skagit House, maybe? Juli shook her head. Not likely, if Shannon had gone somewhere earlier with the Hiltons.

"So they aren't home," she told herself impatiently. "Big deal." She tried again a few times until it got to be too late, then fell asleep, still wondering.

A phone call the next morning got no better results. Neither Shannon nor her father came to church. When

Juli asked Amy if she knew why, the blond girl smiled secretively and said, "Ask her when you see her."

"I will," Juli snapped and walked away. But she didn't get hold of Shannon until late Sunday afternoon. "Where have you been?"

"Here and there," Shannon said after a little silence. Why did she sound so defensive, as if she didn't want to answer Juli's question? "Do you want to come over?" The invitation sounded forced and unnatural. Nothing like her usual, "I'll meet you halfway."

Juli clutched the receiver. "Is anything wrong?"

"Not really. I spent Saturday with Amy. Ted's dad needed him."

"You're acting weird. Is there something I should know?"

"I'm not weird, and what's to know? Are you coming?" Shannon demanded.

"Yes, and I'm going to find out what's happening." Juli put down the phone, pulled down the sleeves of her Hillcrest High Pirates sweatshirt, and headed out.

"Going to Shannon's. Be home before dark." She stepped out into a blooming world of early rhododendrons, crocus, and heavy-budded daffodils. Soon Bellingham would explode with color.

Juli found a small stick and uprooted a spreading dandelion that had dared take root in the Scotts' well-kept lawn. "Good. I'm sick of winter drab." Fresh air and sunlight brightened her mood. She reached the Rileys' brick home, rang the bell, and waited for the rush of steps that meant Shannon was racing downstairs. It didn't happen. Slow, almost timid footsteps crossed the hall. The door opened quietly. "Hi. Let's go out in the backyard. It's nicer there."

Juli blinked. Why on earth should Shannon sound like this? The minute the other girl led the way down the shadowy hall, out the back door, and into the yard, Juli saw the change in her. "Okay, give. What's up?"

"Nothing, really." Shannon's gaze met hers, then slid away. "It's just that it was so wonderful, and you won't understand, and everything is so hard!"

"What are you talking about?" Juli gasped. "What won't I understand, and what's wonderful, and hard?" She dropped into a lawn swing.

Shannon sat down next to her. "I already told you Ted couldn't go with us yesterday. Amy and I drove around some, then she suggested going back to Madame Zelda's." She stared at her fingers. "I told her it was silly, but she said Madame Zelda called her with a message for me, something that concerned my father." Shannon hesitated, then defiantly looked up at Juli. Her laugh sounded unconvincing. "I just wanted to find out what she had to say."

"You actually went back, after—"

"Yes." Shannon squirmed. A faint color came to her pale face. "It wasn't much of a message, just that Dad is lonely and needs to make new friends."

"And a dark, mysterious woman is going to come into

his life," Juli made the mistake of blurting out. A nervous giggle followed.

"Can't you ever be serious? Of course Dad's lonely!" Shannon lashed out. "How would you feel if your father had never come back?" Tears sprang to her eyes but she blinked them back.

"I'm sorry," Juli whispered. "That was really insensitive." What damage had she done by not keeping quiet? "What else did Madame Zelda say?"

"She said there is a small group of people who offer support to those who have lost someone they love. They were meeting Saturday night in one of the downtown buildings. She invited me to come."

Not good. "What about Amy?"

"She was really understanding." Shannon's eyes looked like she had just fully awakened. "She said she'd go with me if I wanted her to. I think we've misjudged her. She said even though there hadn't been a death in her family, it would be nice to know caring people in case it should happen."

"So what are the people at church?" Juli cried. "Chopped liver?"

"I know they're nice, but how much did they really help you?" Shannon asked quietly. "These are people who understand, because of their own losses."

Juli's heart sank. "So you went."

"Yes, and it was wonderful." The Irish girl's face shone. "They started with prayer and Scripture, just like at church. Then their leader, Lord Leopold—"

"Lord Leopold? Who is he?"

"One of the most wonderful men I've ever met," Shannon told her. "He's tall and commanding and wears a plain white robe when he speaks. His name means 'bold for the people.' "

"Are you sure you weren't attending the meeting of some cult?" Juli asked.

"Of course not." Shannon proudly raised her head and squared her shoulders.

Juli would always associate the lonely cry of a night-hawk wheeling through the early evening dusk with the moment she instinctively knew meant far more than she could realize at the time. "What did he say? Lord Leopold, I mean?"

"He talked about how important it is to follow God, even if other people don't accept us," Shannon shared. "He quoted Second Corinthians 6:17, where we are commanded to come out of the world and be separate so God can be our Father." She looked appealingly at Juli. "If you could only have heard him, you'd know how wonderful he is."

"I thought it was supposed to be a meeting to help people with grief."

"It was. I—I went to hear him again this morning," Shannon confessed.

Juli wanted to scream. It might help get rid of the terrible feeling that something was wrong. Instead, she asked,

"Does your father know?"

Shannon shook her head and looked guilty. "No. There was some kind of problem with the alarm system at the bank and he got called in."

"How convenient."

Shannon's face turned scarlet. "That's not fair! You haven't even seen Lord Leopold and you're judging him." She leaped from her chair. "Why did I even bother to try and make you understand? Lord Leopold's right. Those who follow God always have to pay a price. I just never knew it would mean losing my best friend!" Tears streaming, she ran inside and banged the door behind her.

Juli started to follow but thought better of it. What could she say? That the group Shannon had visited was as wonderful as her friend thought? That fear had descended over her the way February fog lowered on Bellingham—heavy, smothering, a blanket no one could throw off? That her insides churned until she wondered if she'd be sick?

Somehow she got home and to her room, unwilling to let Dad and Mom know how upset the visit with Shannon —if it could be called that—had left her. Her fingers itched to dial the Rileys' number, but she shook her head. Not now. Tomorrow would be better, after both girls had time to consider what had happened between them in the lovely yard that turned ugly with accusations.

Juli lay awake for hours, hovering in the gray mists between sleep and reality. A tall, white-shrouded figure moved through her dreams, faceless and terrifying. Not since the nightmares about the gray man had she experienced such dreams. A voice sneered, *"So you're going to write a story about a girl who solves all the bitterness between her family and brother so they can have a happily -ever-after Christmas. Ha! You just lost your best friend. Do you think you can patch things up with ribbons and bows, the way Wendy decorates in your story? No way. It will take a whole lot more than tinsel to undo the damage you did today."*

When the alarm sounded the next morning, all Juli wanted to do was shove her head under the pillows and turn the world to an OFF position. Why hadn't she let God show Shannon the right way, instead of rushing in trying to fix things far too serious to take into her own unskilled hands?

Bone-tired, Juli slid from under the covers. She made sure her door was closed, knelt beside her bed, and began to pray. For herself, asking forgiveness for rushing in "where angels fear to walk," as her friend once misquoted. For Shannon, that she might not be deceived should Lord Leopold and his followers turn out to be false. Amy's face came to mind, so Juli prayed for her, too. Drained, but feeling more at peace, she at last got up and headed for the shower.

# CHAPTER 8

Things did not clear up between Juli and Shannon on Monday. They got even worse on Tuesday. As usual, Amy dropped the bomb. "Guess what! Shannon and I are going to a Spiritual Saturday."

"A what?" Ted choked. He stared at his twin.

"A Spiritual Saturday." Amy calmly popped the tab on a diet soft drink. "The new friends we made over the weekend invited us. Later we may go with them to a retreat. They have grounds near Mount Baker."

Juli looked at Shannon accusingly, but the other girl kept her gaze on her lunch and said nothing. "When did you find out?" Juli casually asked.

Obviously glad to be the center of attention, Amy smiled and said, "They invited us Saturday night at the meeting." She giggled and shot a sideways glance at Dave, then at John Foster, who sat at the end of the table next to Molly. "There are a lot more boys than girls in the group, and are they ever cool!" She rolled her baby blues. "Why don't you go with us, Juli?"

Hurt by the Grand Canyon-size gap yawning between her and Shannon, Juli forgot all about being understanding and letting God work things out. "No way. Only hypocrites attend religious meetings to meet boys."

A shocked silence fell over the lunch group. Shannon's face turned red, then snowy white. She tossed a scornful glance at Amy. "That's not why I'm going. Spiritual Saturday is a time of getting to know yourself and finding out what God wants you to do for Him."

"Sorry."

The unforgiving look in Shannon's eyes didn't change. "Excuse me, please. Coming, Amy?" She got up, grabbed her tray, and marched away. Amy followed, silent for once.

Juli stared at her taco salad with sudden loathing. Why had she ever selected it? And why hadn't she kept her mouth shut?

"Hey, it's not the end of the world." Dave grabbed her hand under the table. "You only said what we were all thinking."

Ted looked as miserable as Juli felt. "Would you believe I had hopes my sister would grow up? Now I'm beginning to wonder." He made a face. "Let's talk about something else."

"Like the fact our basketball team actually won a spot

in the league finals?" John helpfully put in. The boys and Molly immediately began discussing whether the Pirates had a chance in the playoffs. Juli curled her fingers in Dave's hand, thankful for her friends' tactful handling of the unpleasant scene. Yet deep inside she felt like a lost little girl. Having Shannon angry at her was bad enough. Seeing her stubborn, determined expression when she made her own little Declaration of Independence and went off with Amy was the pits.

At the end of a silent, wretched bus ride home, Juli gathered her books and stepped to the sidewalk. Even though she still felt her friend was rushing headfirst into danger, she owed her an apology. Before she could speak, Shannon said in a distant voice, "I'll be driving to school for a while. I'm picking Amy up early. Something's wrong with her Mustang. Anyway, we need to do research."

"Okay." Juli waited for her to say what time she'd be by.

"See you in class." Shannon walked off, her shoulders stiff.

Juli's hopes of straightening things out died. She slowly turned. The ghost of Shannon's laughing presence stalked beside her down the sidewalk the two girls had walked together so often. After making a pretense of eating supper, Juli mumbled, "Homework," and headed for her room. Her books lay unopened. Her story notes mocked her. To her churning brain, even Clue looked at her reproachfully. Juli grabbed a pen, opened her journal, and wrote:

*The saddest word in the world is "over," Lord. If that's all our friendship means to Shannon, it couldn't have been so great, could it?*

Tears splashed to the page. They blurred the ink, but her pen rushed on.

*It's my fault, too. I thought I'd learned I shouldn't try to fix everyone's troubles. I know that's Your job. I'm just so afraid Shannon's getting into something really bad. If not, why is Madame Zelda filling her full of all that garbage about new friends taking the place of the ones she has now?*

Juli stopped writing for a long time. Only by facing her worst fears could she get to a place where she'd be able to look at the whole picture objectively. Maybe she was making too much of small happenings that didn't mean a thing.

*Should I go with Shannon and Amy Saturday, Lord? It scares me silly to even think about it. What if I get hooked? This Lord What's-his-face must really be influential. Shannon's no dummy. She knows the Bible. You said some who pretend to know You are false prophets. Maybe Shannon's right and I have an unreasonable prejudice against people I've never even seen. I have to be honest, Lord. Am I jealous and frightened because I think Amy and this new group may steal Shannon from me?*

She couldn't go on. Laying the journal aside, Juli caught up Clue in her arms, rested her chin on top of his furry head, and rocked back and forth. Undone homework and an unwritten story shouted for her attention. She finally set her stuffed friend back in his usual spot and tackled the homework. The story would have to wait.

Exhausted by the emotionally draining day, Juli overslept. She had to run for the bus, hating the driver's, "Where's your friend?" She wanted to scream when he chuckled. "One of you without the other's like ham without eggs." For a moment, Juli considered telling him intelligent people don't keep repeating themselves and laughing at their stale jokes. She bit her lip. Why take her bad mood out on him? He probably saw enough grouches without her being one.

Wednesday passed. Thursday. Friday. She couldn't stand the strain of a silent Shannon at the lunch table, an even more silent Shannon beside her in the classes they shared. By last period on Friday, Juli came to a major decision. For better or worse—probably the latter, she feared—she had to go with Shannon and Amy on Saturday. Her heart pumped hard. She had trouble breathing, but wrote a note to Shannon and flipped it on her desk. *"If it's still okay, I'll go with you Saturday."* She hastily drew a tiny arrow after the word *"you,"* then inserted *"and Amy"* between the lines.

A look of gratitude crept into the gaze Shannon turned on her. Disappointment followed. She scrawled on the bottom of the page and passed it back to Juli. The letters swam. *"Thanks, but the conference is filled. We had to have our names in by last night. I'm really sorry. Please understand."*

Juli felt someone had dropped a Detour sign on her road to good intentions. She smiled weakly, bursting with impatience for the bell so they could talk.

Of all the times for Mrs. Sorenson to ask Juli to wait after class, why did it have to be today? To top things off, all the teacher wanted was to know how she was coming with her contest story. Juli found it hard to answer with half of her attention still on Shannon. If only she could catch the Irish girl's gaze and motion for her to wait. Just when she thought it might happen, Amy bounced in, destroying any chance of a private talk with Shannon.

That weekend marked another turning point, again for the worse. As early on Sunday morning as she dared, Juli called her friend. Shannon sounded faraway, as if in one short day she had moved back to Ireland. All she said about the Spiritual Saturday was how wonderful it had been and what a fantastic bunch of people attended. "I've never felt so loved," she dreamily reported. "Sorry you couldn't come," she politely added. "Maybe another time."

Juli got the feeling it really didn't matter that much to her. "Will you be at Sunday school and church this morning?"

"I suppose so. Dad's home and I'm not ready to tell him I want to join the Children of Light." Her voice trembled and she sounded more like herself.

"Is that what they're called?"

"Yes. Isn't it wonderful?" Shannon showed enthusiasm for the first time. "Lord Leopold says it is our choice to either walk in darkness or in the light."

"So did Jesus," Juli quickly reminded.

"I know that. Lord Leopold would never preach anything that isn't in the Bible." Shannon sounded faraway again. "I have to rush. See you at church."

Juli hung up, totally frustrated. When she met Shannon and Amy outside the senior high Sunday school classroom, her frustration increased. Amy appeared normal. Not Shannon. A worrisome thought pounded in the back of Juli's brain. Where had she seen the expression now on her friend's face? She concentrated until she had it. Shannon looked like people on TV who had been brainwashed or were coming out of hypnosis. Had she been hypnotized? Drugged?

Chills chased up and down Juli's back. When they went into their classroom, she whispered, "Did you have to take your own lunch yesterday, or did they feed you?"

Shannon's eyes widened with surprise at the seemingly irrelevant question. "They fed us. Sandwiches, potato salad, honey cakes, and Mexican chocolate. They made it the same way Madame Zelda does."

Juli carefully controlled her expression and sat down

next to the others. *Why am I not surprised?* she thought. *I'd give a bundle to get my hands on some of that chocolate and have Dad send it to the police lab for analysis!*

Class went off great except for a small, highly disturbing incident no one seemed to notice but Juli. Their teacher was talking about the need to share the good news that Jesus died to save all those who would believe on Him. Shannon raised her hand. "I have a—a friend who says people spend too much time trying to make everyone believe the way they do," she stated. "He says there shouldn't be competition among the religions of the world—we're all heading for the same place. He says it doesn't matter how we get there. Only the humble will be there, anyway, not the prideful."

Juli felt sick inside, as if she had swallowed a mouthful of poison. *Please, God,* she silently prayed. *Help our teacher know exactly what to say.*

The teacher's keen gaze rested on Shannon's concerned face. "A fair enough question." He smiled at her. "Let's see what Jesus said about it. He's our standard for living. Right?"

"Right." At least Shannon sounded positive about that.

The teacher riffled the pages of his worn Bible. "During what we call the Last Supper, Jesus promised to go and prepare a place for His disciples. He also promised to come back and take them with Him, so they could be where He was. In John 14:4, Jesus says, *'You know the way to the place where I am going.'*

"Thomas, the doubter, who could also be called Thomas the inquisitive, immediately told Jesus they didn't know where He was going. He asked how they could know the way, a question repeated by millions of people since that time. In verse 6, Jesus makes it clear: *'I am the way and the truth and the life. No one comes to the Father except through me.'* " He closed the Bible and smiled again. "Your friend would do well to read those verses, Shannon."

Juli found the palms of her hands soaked with perspiration. Shannon's still-troubled look didn't help. She looked the way she had once described herself: a wishbone, torn two ways. Juli prayed for help.

That afternoon she had a one-person ways and means committee meeting in her bedroom. Did she dare interfere by going to Sean Riley? He had the right to know his daughter was dabbling in some pretty strange stuff, but betrayal could wreck everything between Shannon and Juli. Neither did she feel comfortable talking it over with her own parents. They wouldn't hesitate to take immediate steps if they truly felt Shannon was in danger.

Was she? Or was she only testing the water by bringing up the new teachings from the so-called group therapy sessions in order to get answers? So far, Juli couldn't be sure. Shannon hadn't dropped enough clues to make a case. If only there were a way to find out more about the Children of Light without arousing suspicion! What if she infiltrated the group and pretended to believe what they taught?

Months earlier, Shannon had commented she wished she could hide her feelings and play a role the way Juli did when necessary. Could Juli put her dramatic ability to good use and find out for herself exactly what went on at the meetings presided over by a white-robed man?

The corners of her mouth turned down. Dad's trained eyes would see right through her vague excuses about where she was going and when. Sean Riley kept a check on Shannon, but simply assumed when she wasn't home or at school that she was at the Scotts'. Juli's folks wanted more details concerning their daughter's activities.

"Maybe I can get one of the boys to do it," she confided to Clue. "John is pretty levelheaded. Ted?" She shook her head. "With Amy and Shannon so involved, he's too close to the problem and might not be able to stay objective. Dave would be better." She remembered how Scott and Gilmore, P.I.s, as Dave called them, worked together on *Mysterious Monday*, their first case. Smart, caring, dependable, able to keep his mouth shut, Dave was the perfect partner for Juli Scott, Super Sleuth, and not just because he was her boyfriend.

"I'll ask him," Juli told Clue. "As soon as the basketball play-offs are over." A trickle of fear went through her. "I hope I'm not putting him in danger. What if he's as vulnerable as Shannon?" She shook her head until her blondish-brown hair swished. "He won't be! He will already know what to expect, like that the Mexican chocolate may be drugged. He can be a lot more careful than Shannon."

No matter how many times Juli reassured herself, the fear remained. Did she have the right to ask Dave for the help she strongly felt he'd be glad to give? Back and forth, back and forth, went her thoughts. She finally decided the risk was too great and regretfully gave up her scheme.

A few days later, everything changed. Ted Hilton cornered Juli the instant she stepped down from the bus. His blue eyes looked enormous. "Do you know what's wrong with Shannon?" he demanded.

"Why?" Dread swept through Juli.

"She's losing it." The good-natured basketball player ran one hand over his close-cropped, light brown hair. "We hung out at her place for a while last night, then hit the closest Burger King." The bell rang, but Ted and Juli didn't move.

"So what happened?"

His tanned face whitened. "You won't believe it," he warned. "On the way home, Shannon got this kind of glittery look in her eyes and started crying."

"Go on!" Juli almost screamed.

Ted looked sick. "She said I was the only one who really cared about her. Juli, she asked me to elope."

# CHAPTER 9

Juli felt the blood drain from her face. She stared at Ted, unable to believe her own ears. "Shannon asked you to elope? As in *getting married?*"

Ted nodded and said hoarsely, "That's what I said."

"Sixteen-year-old girls don't elope." Juli felt like the earth had caved in beneath her feet. "At least, not ones like Shannon."

"I know that," Ted exclaimed. "Don't you see? It shows how serious whatever's bothering her really is. She'd never ask me or any other guy to marry her unless she felt it was the only way out." He clenched his hands and pain twisted his face. "The question is, way out of what? How can she be in trouble bad enough to drive her to the point of desperation? Where's it coming from? The horoscope stuff and fortune-teller Amy tried to shove down our throats?"

"Maybe."

"So what do we do now?"

"I don't know. What did you say? You don't have to answer," she added.

Ted turned red. "You might as well know all of it. I told her the truth." His honest blue gaze locked with Juli's. "She's the best thing that ever happened to me. If she's around six years from now when we both finish college, things may work out. They sure won't if we jump into marriage when we're sixteen years old! Shannon stared at me for a minute then said, 'You're probably right.' She sounded totally defeated, but what could I do? I walked her to the door, waited until she got inside, then went home. I didn't sleep much."

"Have you seen her this morning?"

He shook his head and looked uncomfortable. "I don't know what to say to her. I didn't dump Shannon, but she acted like I had. Do girls feel this rotten when they dump guys?"

"I don't know. I've never dumped anyone."

"Me neither." Ted gave her a twisted grin. "You're her best friend, Juli, or I'd never have told you what happened. Keep it to yourself, okay? *I'm* sure not going to say anything."

"Of course. You don't think Shannon will tell Amy, do you?"

"I hope not." Ted growled. "She might as well announce it on the PA system." He glanced at the empty steps leading up to the school. "I don't think I'll go to first period class. It's almost over, and I need some time. Uh. . .thanks."

"Any time," she told him, then went up the steps and inside, knowing she had to put on the performance of her life when she saw Shannon.

Juli needn't have worried. Shannon didn't come to school, at least not to classes the girls shared. Ted met Juli at her locker when the final bell ended the longest day Juli could remember. "Not here, right? Amy doesn't know where she is. She said Shannon was fine when she picked her up yesterday morning. Amy had cheerleading practice after school, so they didn't go home together."

"So whatever happened to make her so desperate had to be between the end of school and when you got to her place last night," Juli reasoned. "Are you going to see her?"

"I can't." Worry lines wrinkled Ted's smooth face. "There are only a few days left until the basketball play-offs. Coach Barrett will throw me off the team if I miss practice. How about you?"

"I'll stop by on the way home," Juli promised.

"Thanks." Ted gave her a weak smile and ran down the hall.

All the way home on the bus, Juli wondered how to approach Shannon. Gone were the days when she could simply bounce in, park on a chair or the bed and demand, "Okay, what's wrong with you?" Would those days ever return? The thought depressed Juli. Just a few weeks ago, if anyone had told her she and Shannon would ever let something come between them, she'd have laughed. Now it took every ounce of patience she possessed to smile at the bus driver's usual routine when she got off the bus. She turned toward the Rileys' instead of home. The short distance felt like miles. When Juli got there, she wished it had been longer. "Please, God," she whispered. "Help me know what to say."

She rang the bell and waited. No one came. She rang again. On the third try, the heavy carved front door opened a few inches. "Shannon?"

"Hi, Juli." Shannon's eyes looked dull, but huge in her pale face. "Come in." She opened the door wider.

Juli stepped into the hall and stared at her friend. "You're sick?"

"Uh-huh." Shannon staggered into the living room and lay down on the couch. "I woke up this morning feeling awful. By the time I got dressed, I felt headachy and cold." She shivered and pulled an afghan over her body, even though the room must have been in the high 70s. "Some kind of bug, I guess."

*Oh? A virus wouldn't have made you ask Ted to elope last night,* Juli thought. *If only I can find out where you were between school and when he came by.* "You sure got away fast after honors writing class yesterday," she commented.

"Did you want me for something?" Shannon sounded like it didn't matter, like nothing mattered.

Juli frantically searched for a reason. "How are you coming with the revisions on 'Katie'?" Not fantastic, but the best she could come up with at the moment. "We don't have that long before the deadline."

"I'm not going to enter the contest."

"Not enter? How come?" Juli recognized the defeat in Shannon's voice that Ted had described from the night before.

Shannon closed her eyes. Her lashes looked extra dark against her white cheeks. "Lord Leopold says Christians need to guard against pride."

This time, Juli refused to allow the hot words just behind her to teeth come out. Instead of condemning the leader, she said, "Pastor Johnson said in one of his sermons it's okay to be proud of our abilities. We just need to do our best and recognize our talents are from God, not from ourselves."

Shannon didn't answer, so Juli went on. "The team's practicing harder than ever for the basketball play-offs." Should she ask Shannon to go with her? She took a deep breath, held it, then blew out. "I hope you're feeling better by then."

"I won't be going, even if I'm better. There's a special Children of Light therapy session the first night of the play-offs." Her eyes opened, but she didn't look at Juli. "I wouldn't want to skip that just for a basketball game." She pulled the afghan higher.

Juli couldn't play it cool any longer. She knelt beside the couch. "Shannon, I am really worried about you." She laid one hand on her friend's forehead. "This room is hot, but you say you're freezing." She laid her head on the other girl's head. "You're burning up! Does your dad know you're sick?"

"No. He mustn't! He won't let me go to the meeting." Terror came to Shannon's eyes. She pushed Juli away and struggled to a sitting position.

"What are you afraid of?" Juli cried. She grabbed Shannon's arms and forced her back into a lying down position.

"Who's afraid of the Big Bad Wolf?" Shannon croaked. Her eyes glittered and twin red spots burned on her cheeks.

The sweetest sound in the world to Juli was the rattle of a key in the lock. Thank God! "In here!" she called. "Shannon's sick."

Sean Riley strode into the room and to the couch. "What happened?"

"She didn't come to school today so I stopped by. I found her like this."

"Get the thermometer from the medicine cabinet in the bathroom," he ordered. Juli ran to get it. Shannon's temperature registered 102.5.

"Call and see if Dr. Marlowe is still in her office," Sean told Juli. "If so, ask her if she will wait for us. If she isn't available, call the hospital and tell them we're bringing Shannon into Emergency."

"Dad!" Shannon raised up on one elbow. "I'll be fine."

*She wants to go to that meeting,* Juli thought. *Over my dead body!*

"Make the call, Juli," the banker said.

"I will." *Please be there,* she prayed, waiting for the call to go through.

A crisp voice answered, "Dr. Marlowe's office. May I help you?"

"This is Juli Scott, calling for Sean Riley. Shannon's running a temperature of 102.5," Juli breathlessly reported. "Is it okay to bring her in?"

"Just a moment, please." After a time on hold that felt like centuries, the nurse said, "Dr. Marlowe says bring her right in. She'll wait."

"Thanks." Juli hung up and told Sean, "I'll go with you."

"Call your father and let him know where you'll be," he said.

Juli did, then helped him get a still-protesting Shannon into the back seat of the Riley van where she could lie down. Juli crawled into the front seat beside Sean, hurting inside. "What do you think it is?"

"I'd guess a virus and mild dehydration, but we won't take chances." Sean concentrated on navigating the evening commuter traffic rush. "I'm just glad you stopped by." He sent a lightning glance at her before returning his attention to the wheel. In a voice that wouldn't carry even to the back seat he asked, "Juli, is something wrong between you and Shannon?"

Torn between concern and loyalty, all she could say was, "I hope not. We did have a—a kind of argument."

"I know she's been hanging out with Amy a lot lately. She also spoke of some new friends. Do you know them?"

"No." Juli had never felt more grateful than when they swung into the parking lot at the clinic where Dr. Marlowe practiced. Another minute or two and she'd spill all her worry and anger, something she just wasn't ready to do at this point.

Shannon continued to say she was okay, but her father overruled her. "We'll let Dr. Marlowe decide that." He and Juli took her inside.

Dr. Marlowe met them in the empty waiting room. Even the nurse had gone home. "All right, Shannon, let's take a look at you." She led the sick girl into another room. Juli heard her say, "Slip into this gown and I'll be right back. I just want to talk with your father and Juli."

Dr. Marlowe came back smiling. "I doubt it's anything serious, but you're wise to check." She glanced at a chart. "Any changes since I gave Shannon her sports physical last fall? Is she taking medication?" The doctor laughed. "She's not into diet pills or anything, is she?"

"Not that I know of." Sean slipped into a bit of brogue. "Heaven knows she's not for needin' to lose weight. Juli?"

She chose her words carefully. An accusation that Madame Zelda might be lacing hot chocolate with a dangerous substance could not be made without proof. "Neither of us takes diet pills and she isn't on medication," she said.

"Good." Dr. Marlowe smiled at her, leaving Juli with the insane urge to fling herself into the doctor's arms and cry. Only the knowledge that such behavior would open up the need for more explanations than she dared give saved her from humiliating herself.

Dr. Marlowe vanished into the examining room. Juli excused herself to use the restroom. She dawdled as long as she dared, dodging the chance of more questions from Sean Riley. By the time she worked up courage to face him, she heard the examining room door open. Juli timed her return for just after Dr. Marlowe and Shannon reached the waiting room.

Her friend sat slumped in a chair, looking so defenseless, Juli wanted to put her arms around her and whisper everything would be all right. She knew better. Right now, all she could do was stand by and pray that whatever had attacked her friend's body and mind would be lifted. Soon.

Dr. Marlowe gave the exact diagnosis Sean had predicted. "Probably a twenty-four-hour virus, plus mild dehydration." She handed Shannon a small foil pouch. "I prefer my patients under eighteen stick with nonaspirin products. These capsules will reduce the fever.

"It's critical that you drink, drink, drink! Water and fruit juice, for the most part. Soft drinks are all right, but don't skimp on the water. Stay home from school until Monday and get plenty of rest." Her eyes twinkled. "Be nice to yourself. You're worth it!"

Juli finally got home and told her concerned parents Shannon would be fine. "What's for dinner, or did I miss it?"

"We waited, and it's my special lasagna," Dad proudly told her.

"Good. I have to make a call, then I'll be right back," Juli promised. She headed for the den and called Ted, wishing she had a separate line to her room.

"Can I see Shannon?" he wanted to know.

"Not tonight. Dr. Marlowe ordered her to go to bed as soon as she got home." Juli hesitated. "Anyway, do you think that's a good idea after last night?"

"Probably not." Ted sounded totally down. "How about flowers and a card?"

"She'll love them. Tell Amy, will you? Dinner's ready and I'm starving."

"Sure. Uh, Juli, should I have Mom put her on the church prayer chain?"

"Not unless it's a lot more serious than Dr. Marlowe thinks." She said good-bye, ate dinner, stood under a warm shower for a long time, and crawled into bed with Clue in her arms. This was one night she needed all the rest she could get. Exhaustion did its work well. She fell asleep before she finished her prayers.

A short visit the next day after school found Shannon much improved. "I feel like a fake," she complained. "Temperature's down, and except for being a little weak, I could do an Irish jig. Don't worry," she added when Juli glared at her. "I'll be good. Look what Ted sent." She nodded at a huge bouquet of wildflowers. "Mercy me, the lad must be for tryin' to impress me."

Juli's knees threatened to give way beneath her. It had been weeks since Shannon had lapsed into an Irish accent. "I'm glad you're feeling so much better."

"I'd be even better if I weren't so fuzzy." Shannon rubbed her eyes. "Ted was here and we went out for shakes. I remember stumbling up to my room after he brought me home. I woke up feeling terrible."

All Juli could get out was, "Fever does funny things, doesn't it?" So funny Shannon didn't remember asking Ted to elope!

"I guess." She yawned. "I don't understand how anything so small as a virus can totally wipe out a person. It's all I can do to stay awake."

"I'll get out of here and let you rest," Juli told her. "See you."

"See you," Shannon sleepily echoed. But when Juli reached the door, Shannon added, "I'm really glad you came."

Juli's heart jumped with happiness. "So am I." She ran all the way home, thanking God with every step. Good was supposed to come out of everything. Well, with Shannon sick, she wouldn't be going to some meeting!

On Sunday night, Shannon called to say she'd be by for Juli the next morning. She didn't say one word about all the days she'd picked up Amy and Juli had taken the bus. Neither did Juli. Being friends again was more important than dwelling on the past.

Morning came bright and beautiful, making Juli feel what she labeled "springish." She slid into a blue T-shirt and matching print skirt. "It's so nice, I'll wait on the porch," she decided. Lost in happy thoughts, she paid little attention to the time until Dad stepped outside.

"You still here? How come?"

"Shannon's picking me up." Juli glanced at her watch. "Uh-oh. She's late."

"Better call her."

Juli raced inside and dialed. She got the answering machine.

"Any luck?" Dad said from the doorway.

"No, and now I've missed the bus! Will you take me, please?"

"Of course." He frowned. "You don't think she had a relapse, do you?"

Juli thought of Shannon's recent mood swings and forgetfulness. She sniffed. "More likely she forgot me and went with Amy." She ignored Dad's quick glance, folded her arms, and silently stared out the window all the way to school.

# CHAPTER 10

Hurt and confused by Shannon's failure to show up, Juli deliberately avoided her group of church friends and sneaked into her first class. Her head ached and she found it impossible to concentrate, so she called home at the end of class. "I don't feel good, Dad. Will you please come get me?"

"Be right there. Hope you haven't caught Shannon's bug."

"Me, too." Juli hung up and slowly walked to her locker for her books. She hadn't lied. She really did feel sick, although she hadn't caught anything from Shannon except more disappointment. Why not forget her and get on with her own life? *Because Shannon wouldn't give up on you,* her conscience reminded.

"Okay, so I'll hang in there," Juli muttered. As soon

as she and Dad got home, she took something for her headache and headed for bed. If only she could sleep and block out all her problems!

Juli's wish came true. She didn't awaken until that afternoon when Dad knocked on her door and called, "Juli, there's someone here to see you."

She came alive in a hurry. "Is it Shannon?"

"No. It's a Mr. Fred Halvorsen."

"Fred Halvorsen? I don't know a Fred Halvorsen." Swiping at her hair with a brush, she fastened her robe and slid her feet into thongs.

"He knows you. And Shannon." Dad sounded dead serious.

A twinge of anxiety went through Juli. She flung open her bedroom door and followed Gary Scott down the hall to the living room. A good-natured man who looked strangely unfamiliar without his uniform and usual smile got up from a chair.

"Why, it's our bus driver! Funny. I never knew your name."

Mr. Halvorsen's lips twitched. "Most people don't." He waited until she and her father sat down then dropped back into his chair. "I hope you don't feel I'm interfering. I'll feel pretty stupid if it turns out to be nothing, but I've been thinking about something all day. Besides, after I got off work and told my wife, she said I should report what happened to someone."

He shifted uneasily and looked at Gary Scott. "I've

driven this route enough to know you're a policeman. I figured you'd decide whether to check it out."

"Check what out, Mr. Halvorsen?" Dad changed from friendly to all business.

"Well, like I always tell the girls, seeing one without the other is like ham without eggs. I know you haven't been together as much lately. Shannon waves at me mornings from that blue Honda she's been driving. That's how I knew who it was today." He looked appealingly at Juli.

*Must he ramble on and on? Why doesn't he get to the point?* Juli's nails dug into the palms of her hands and she willed him to continue.

An uneasy look chased across Fred Halvorsen's cheerful countenance. "It's probably nothing, but there's so much devilment going on these days, my wife and I don't feel right about not speaking up. Anyway, this morning Shannon was at the stop sign in her Honda, just up from where the girls usually board my bus. She was wearing her red ski jacket. Kind of surprised me, 'cause it was such a nice morning. Well, a man and woman crossed the street in front of her then walked to the car. Shannon smiled and rolled down the window.

"They said something to her. Naturally, I couldn't hear what. I got busy with the folks getting on the bus. By the time I looked again, the man was in the passenger's seat and the woman just behind him." Mr. Halvorsen scratched his head. "Shannon took off, faster than I've ever seen her drive, but she gave me a funny look before she did. She didn't wave or anything, just stared at me."

"Did she look frightened?"

The driver chewed on a thumbnail. "That's why I decided I'd better come see you folks. At the time, I didn't think much about it, except to wonder how come she stared at me, but didn't wave. The more I thought about it, the more I decided maybe she was scared. Or maybe worried. I suppose the man and woman could have been her parents bringing bad news, but why would they come from that direction?" Bewilderment on his face showed how mixed-up he felt.

"Her mother's dead. Maybe it was Mr. Riley and the cleaning woman." Juli didn't believe her explanation for one minute.

Mr. Halvorsen shook his head so violently his round cheeks shook. "Cleaning woman? Not on your life! Nobody cleans house in clothes that look like they just came out of some high-priced store."

A terrible hollowness formed in Juli's stomach. "Can you describe her?"

"Sure. Dark-skinned. I wondered if she might be a foreigner." He grinned sheepishly. "You'll probably laugh, but all I could think was, if she'd been dressed in bright colors instead of black, she'd have made a good gypsy."

"What did the man look like?" Dad asked. A muscle twitched in his cheek.

"He could have been anyone. Tall. Dark suit. Briefcase. I see commuters like him by the dozens." An anxious look came into the driver's eyes. "You don't think anything bad has happened to the little gal, do you?"

"Probably not, but I really appreciate your taking the time to contact me," Dad told him. "Concerned citizens like you make police officers' jobs a lot easier. I'm on leave from the force right now, but I'll certainly look into it." He shook hands with the man, walked to the porch with him, chatted for a few moments, then came back to where a white-faced Juli huddled on the couch. He dropped into a chair. "All right. Start talking. From the beginning, and don't leave anything out." His keen gray gaze bored into her.

"Got it, Dad." Juli felt so glad circumstances were forcing her to tell, she would have cheered if it hadn't been for the raw fear inside her. "You were there when it started. No, it was before that." Her mind raced back to the Tuesday lunch when Amy had brought the daily horoscope to the cafeteria table.

"You aren't making sense, Juli. Settle down and start over."

The truth, every word of it, came out in painful bits and pieces. Shannon's fascination with Amy's horoscope and the coincidence of the blond cheerleader receiving word of her inheritance just then. Amy's pressure on Shannon to visit Madame Zelda. Juli's refusal to go with her. The Mexican chocolate, crystal ball, seemingly uncanny predictions. "I thought when we put them on paper, Shannon accepted that anyone who cared to do a little research could find out those things," Juli said brokenly. "We got back

together and she acted normal again. I guess I was wrong."
She bit her lip. "I got really busy with my story for the magazine contest and didn't spend much time with Shannon. We had company coming on Saturday and I couldn't hang out with her when she asked me to.

"That night I called her a gazillion times. She didn't answer or come to church the next morning. I went over to her place in the afternoon. Dad, it was awful!"

"Awful in what way?" Gary Scott leaned forward, arms rigid.

Juli felt the same frustration she had then. "Madame Zelda sent word by Amy. She supposedly had a message about Shannon's dad. Naturally, Shannon went to find out what it was. Some message." She glared. "Just that Sean is lonely and needs to make new friends."

Her father only grunted.

"Madame Zelda also told Shannon about this wonderful support group for those who have lost someone they love. I didn't realize how much Shannon is still grieving for her mother." Juli fell quiet for a time. "She and Amy went that night and again the next morning."

Dad interrupted her story. "Who are these people?"

"They call themselves the Children of Light. A Lord Leopold, which means 'bold for the people,' wears a white robe, quotes Scripture, and preaches, as well as doing therapy sessions. Shannon says he's tall, commanding, and one of the most wonderful men she's ever met," Juli said bitterly.

"What does he preach?" The question cracked like a whip in the quiet room.

"That's what worries me." She stared at her hands. "He keeps talking about having to leave everyone behind who doesn't understand. I don't have a clue what that's supposed to mean. Anyway, they're supposed to sacrifice for God by separating themselves from friends and family in order to come closer to Him."

"Dangerous teachings," Dad said quietly. "Go on, Juli."

It felt so good just to be able to pour out everything that troubled her! "Shannon blew up and ran out. I came home. She started picking Amy up mornings and doing things with her. They went to some kind of 'Spiritual Saturday' meeting. Shannon told me at church on Sunday she'd never felt so loved. She wanted to join the Children of Light, but didn't know how to tell her dad. She acted like her body was at church and her mind in outer space."

"Is there any chance she took or was given a drug?"

"She'd never take drugs. I've wondered if someone gave her something without her knowing it."

"Why?"

Juli tried to sort facts from reality. "Madame Zelda served Mexican chocolate. Shannon drank two cups, then felt drowsy, but the room was warm.

"The Children of Light served the same kind of Mexican chocolate at their meeting. Shannon acted strange afterwards, but she might have anyway, since she knew I didn't approve of her going.

"A few days later, Shannon went somewhere between school and the time Ted got to her house that evening. On the way home from Burger King, she. . ." Juli remembered her promise to Ted just before blurting out that Shannon had asked him to elope. "She started acting totally weird. Only she missed school the next day and I found her sick, so that may explain it." She reluctantly added, "At least her being sick didn't have anything to do with drugs. Dr. Marlowe said she had a touch of twenty-four-hour flu and got dehydrated from not drinking enough fluids."

"No drug problem there," Dad admitted. He stood and paced the floor. "How could you keep this to yourself, Juli, even if a lot of it may just be suspicion? If these people really are messing with Shannon's mind, or giving her drugs, she's in danger."

"I wanted to tell you!" Juli cried. "I just couldn't. You're supposed to stay away from anything stressful. I also knew you'd tell Shannon's father. She'd find out. Shannon is my best friend and was already slipping away from me. I knew she'd never forgive me for getting her into trouble."

Dad's face didn't relax. "How stressful do you think it will be for me, and all of us, if something happens to Shannon?" He paced again, then sat back down beside her. "Don't you know false loyalty, refusing to tell those who need to know and can help, may lead to situations that get out of control, even kill? Juli, I want you to remember this for the rest of your life: It's easier to live with losing a friendship than knowing you could have prevented losing a friend."

"I'll remember, Dad. I'm sorry," she choked out. Her stomach rolled. She jumped up and made it to the bathroom just in time. Weak and miserable, she clung to Dad's free hand while he wiped her hot face with a cool, damp washcloth. For a moment, she felt five years old again, with Dad taking care of her because Mom was sick also.

"I hate to ask you to go on," he said quietly. "However, I do need to know everything, no matter how insignificant it seems."

"All right." Juli obediently followed him back to the living room. "It doesn't excuse me, but since Shannon got over being sick, there's been a big change. She laughs a lot, the way she used to. Sometimes she talks in an Irish brogue again."

"Anything else?"

"That time with Ted is pretty fuzzy."

"Not conclusive, since she came down with something the next day."

Juli rubbed her forehead, feeling drained. "Are you going to call the police?"

Dad looked serious. "Not yet. We can't assume there's been a crime."

"Mr. Halvorsen was concerned enough to come tell us what he saw!"

"Right. I'm glad he did. I also have to ask myself, what did he see?" Dad ticked off what they knew on his fingers. "*One:* Shannon at the stop sign. *Two:* a man and woman she obviously knows, because she smiles when they come to the car. *Three:* the people in the car. *Four:* Shannon failing to wave. *Five:* the Honda driving away."

"You left out some things," she protested. "What about Shannon looking scared and taking off faster than usual?"

"There's enough distance between the bus stop and the stop sign that Mr. Halvorsen could be mistaken. Remember, he said he didn't decide she looked that way until later, chiefly based on the fact she didn't wave. Shannon could have been thinking about the friends in her car."

"If they were friends," Juli put in. "That woman sounds suspiciously like Madame Zelda, and I don't trust her."

"Not trusting her doesn't make her a kidnapper," Dad reminded.

The hideous word fell into the room like a bomb. Even though Juli disagreed with Dad about what the driver had seen, she hadn't allowed the thought of kidnapping to take root in her mind. Mouth dry, she stared at her father. "You aren't ruling out the possibility, are you." A statement, not a question.

"No, Juli." Dad's strong hand dropped to her tightly clenched ones. His kind eyes held sadness. "We both know it can happen. Yet the best thing we can do until we make sure is to pray, and believe Shannon isn't a victim. If she is, I promise I will do everything in my power to find and help her." He squeezed her hands and glanced at his watch. "Shannon should be getting home from school about now. Give her a call. If you get the answering machine, just say you didn't feel well and came home. Ask her to call when she receives the message."

Heart thumping, Juli obeyed, desperately praying for Shannon to answer. The answering machine clicked on. Juli left her message, hung up, and waited. Before Mom arrived, the phone rang twice. A charity wanted a donation. A company wanted to clean the Scotts' carpet. Juli wanted to scream!

Anne Scott came home to a sober household. She looked sick when they filled her in. A little after six, the phone rang. Juli couldn't move. Dad answered. "Hello? Sean? Shannon's staying with a friend tonight? Thanks. I'll tell Juli."

She should feel relieved. She should laugh at her wild imagination and apologize to Dad and Mom for getting so upset. Juli couldn't. The alarm triggered by Mr. Halvorsen's visit refused to stop clanging in her brain. Sean Riley's logical explanation had two gaping holes. It didn't explain (a) why Shannon didn't pick Juli up, after she herself set the time and their friendship was just getting back to normal, or (b) why she hadn't called to apologize for not showing.

# Chapter 11

Shannon Riley braked, brought her blue Honda to a stop at the corner, and waited for a break in the heavy traffic so she could make a left turn. It felt so neat to be on her way to Juli's again! Shannon shivered, glad for the warmth of her ski jacket, even on this gloriously sunny morning. She must still be run-down from the flu. It didn't take much for her to chill.

She sighed. *At least time off from school gave me time to think. A lot. How could I be stupid enough to let a difference of opinion nearly destroy a friendship? Thanks for fixing things, God. I know when Juli meets Lord Leopold and the Children of Light, she'll see how wrong she is about them. Madame Zelda, too. They really love You, and do they ever know the Bible!*

A happy smile curved her lips and a warm glow went

through her. In just a few minutes, Juli would slide in beside her, dark blue eyes glowing with excitement over the simple fact they were back where they belonged—together. "Me, too, God," Shannon whispered. "Thanks again."

Out of the corner of her eye, Shannon saw the bus coming down the street toward the stop a short distance away. She grinned. Since she'd been picking Amy up early, she missed the friendly driver's stale greeting! Shame for not inviting Juli to ride along with her and Amy scorched Shannon. "You only hurt the ones who love you," she soberly misquoted, forgetting Juli had corrected her Rileyism by saying the classic song title was, "You Only Hurt the One You Love."

"Never again," she vowed. "No matter what, I'll never hurt Juli again."

A black-clad man and an elegantly dressed woman stepped from the opposite curb, crossed the street, and came toward her car. Could that be. . .yes!

Shannon rolled down her window and smiled at Lord Leopold and Madame Zelda. "Hello. What are you doing in my neighborhood?"

"Good morning, Shannon. We need to talk with you. May we get in?"

Surprised at the coldness of the greeting, she replied, "Of course." Why should a little quiver dim some of the day's brightness? Shannon ignored it and unlatched the doors she always kept locked while driving. Lord Leopold took her backpack from the seat, laid it on the floor, and slid in beside her. Madame Zelda got into the back seat. "Is something wrong?" Shannon asked.

"That depends on you." Leopold's colorless eyes held no warmth. "Why didn't you come to the Children of Light meeting last Sunday?"

She looked away from the penetrating stare and pulled her ski jacket closer around her. "I—I went to church. I haven't told my father I want to change."

"Why not? Don't you know God expects us to leave all and follow Him?"

Shannon's hands tightened on the steering wheel. "It's so hard."

"Jesus makes it clear in Luke 14:26. *'If anyone comes to me and does not hate his father and mother, his wife and children, his brothers and sisters—yes, even his own life— he cannot be my disciple,'* " the relentless voice went on.

"What kind of God demands such a thing?" Shannon protested.

Madame Zelda leaned forward and placed one hand on Shannon's shoulder. "He's love. Don't you feel it when you are with the Children of Light?"

"Of course." Memory of the warmth that surrounded her, the feeling nothing in the world mattered except being with those who understood her because they had suffered also, made Shannon's voice tremble.

The woman went on. "God is not trying to punish us. He simply knows we cannot walk in that light if we allow ourselves to be distracted. Anything worth having requires sacrifice." Her voice took on a warning note. "Why do you find it so hard to yield your will? Surely you aren't arrogant enough to believe you know better than God what is needed in your life!"

"Come with us, Shannon," Lord Leopold told her. "Walk among the Children of Light and be a beacon in a world of darkness. Madame Zelda has seen and told you of the joy in store for you if you have faith to follow in the true way." He looked deep into her eyes. She felt herself drowning in the colorless depths and broke the spell by tearing her gaze from his.

"We understand how you are feeling," Lord Leopold went on. "Have I myself not become a pilgrim and stranger, a man pointed out and scorned for daring to follow the path God has set before me? Have I not cried over a hundred, nay, a thousand souls like you, souls God is calling to rise up and stand for Him? Have I not known agony and despair over the lost lamb who cannot find its way, even while my heart rejoices over the ninety-nine safely in the fold?"

His words beat on Shannon like hailstones. The sadness in his voice did what no amount of reasoning could accomplish. When Lord Leopold took her hand in his gloved one and quietly said, "You are being asked to choose this day, Shannon," she felt the resistance draining out of her. Yet enough doubt remained to make her say, "I can't just go. I have to turn a story in to my writing teacher. I told Juli I would pick her up, and—"

An ominous whisper came from the back seat. "If you value your friend, you will go with us. Now."

"What!" Shannon whipped around and stared at Madame Zelda.

"Silence!" Lord Leopold turned to face the fortune-teller. Shannon stared. His face looked as if an ugly devil mask had dropped over it. The next instant his expression changed. "She means after you become one of us, you'll be able to show your friend the truth."

His explanation came one terrifying moment too late. No one called of God could carry such a look of hate in his eyes. *Lord, help me,* Shannon silently cried. "You said to choose, so I will." She lapsed into brogue. "I'll not be for goin' with you, now or ever." Shannon felt chains she hadn't realized bound her break and fall away. "Please get out of my car." She saw an angry gleam come to Lord Leopold's eyes.

A dismayed gasp came from behind her. "You can't mean that!"

Strength far beyond her own flowed through Shannon. "I can and I do. Get out of my car and out of my life!"

"Do you think we've wasted all this time on you only to let some whim take you away?" A crafty look crept into Leopold's face. He glanced up and down the street. "There's a halt in the traffic. Make a right turn and keep going until I give you further directions."

Shannon folded her arms over her ski jacket and said, "Nothing you can do will make me go with you. Juli was right. You're phonies, both of you."

Something hard poked into her back. "Don't look around," Leopold said. "Madame is an excellent shot. Perhaps you should turn left instead of right. I believe you said your friend was waiting for you?"

Like the replay of a familiar song came Shannon's vow from just a short while ago. *No matter what, I'll never hurt Juli again.* Better to sacrifice herself than get Juli involved in this mess. Senses made keen by the danger she knew swirled around them both, Shannon desperately tried to figure a way to signal someone, anyone. She cast an agonized look at her bus driver friend, hoping the distance between wouldn't disguise the fact she was in trouble. He looked surprised when she released the brake and stepped on the gas, but common sense said it could be her imagination. The Honda swung into a right turn with a screech of tires. The driver waved. Shannon gritted her teeth and kept both hands on the wheel. Not much of a clue, but the best she could manage. Shaking inside, but more alert than she had ever been in her life, Shannon forced herself to say, "If you are kidnapping me, I need to go home and get some clothes."

"Kidnapping is a harsh word, but it doesn't apply to those who come willingly." Leopold sounded amused. "If necessary, we will testify you wanted to join the Children of Light. Once away from disturbing influences, you'll soon become one of us. Of course, you will need clothes and you'll leave a message on the answering machine that you're staying with a friend. Don't forget your cash card if you don't have it with you." He calmly picked up her back-pack and pawed through it. "Not here. Drive home, but don't get any funny ideas."

"How do you know I have a cash card?" Shannon gasped.

"Madame Zelda has a way of gaining information without persons realizing it. Especially from silly little girls like your friend."

"*Amy* told you?"

"But of course." Madame Zelda laughed triumphantly. "She told me all about the Irish girl into whose capable hands Sean Riley places both confidence and the running of their home to teach her responsibility. Naturally, this daughter needs money for groceries and paying bills. Her banker father easily obtained the bank manager's approval for a joint checking account and cash cards."

Lord Leopold joined in the laughter. "You need to withdraw a contribution to the Children of Light. If you prefer, you can consider it money for room and board. Periodically, you will write and ask your father to deposit more money in your account. So much more effective and less risky than having to arrange for a cash delivery when needed."

"Ransom."

"Not at all." He chuckled. "Just a loving father helping support a daughter who wants to get away for a time and doesn't believe it is right to expect friends to pay for her needs. We wouldn't want him to suspect anything else."

*They must have been planning this for weeks,* Shannon

had time to think before she turned the corner and pulled up in front of her home. She tried a bluff. "What am I supposed to tell the cleaning woman about not being in school? She's going to wonder who you are and what you're doing here."

"Nice try. She doesn't come on Mondays." Lord Leopold stepped out of the car and walked with her to the front door. Shannon's shaking fingers refused to fit the key into the keyhole. He helped her, then said, "I wouldn't try to stall long enough to set off the alarm system. Your friend will still be waiting for you."

"I wasn't considering it," she said truthfully. She hadn't thought about the alarm going off until Leopold suggested it.

He followed her upstairs to her bedroom. "There's no need to be frightened. I'm perfectly willing to put this unpleasantness behind us. After all, Satan plants rebellion in people's hearts and God expects us to forgive."

Shannon had the insane desire to laugh. A warning voice inside her said she must not. Lord Leopold actually believed himself called of God to lead the Children of Light. This made him even more dangerous. Tragedies occurred among groups of people who put too much faith in their leader. Thankfulness took away some of her numbness. She'd come so close to being one of those who blindly accepted Lord Leopold's teachings!

*I might be forced to stay with the Children of Light for a time,* she silently admitted. *The best way to survive may be in pretending to go along with them. It might take away their suspicions and give me a chance to escape. If I do, I'll have to go far away, so far they can't find me. That way there won't be any reason for them to hurt Juli.*

"Nothing fancy," her captor ordered after she found her cash card and turned to the closet. "Warm clothing. Heavy shoes. Toilet articles."

Shannon decided she might as well start cooperating, and did as she was told.

Back in the car, Lord Leopold directed Shannon through the streets and commanded her to pull up in front of a branch of her father's bank, but not the one where Sean Riley worked. "Draw out three hundred dollars," Leopold said. "That's reasonable for a couple of weeks room and board."

Shannon obeyed. If it weren't for Juli, she'd scream her head off. Or drive to the nearest police station. Or do anything except be part of this nightmare. Hope filled her. Maybe that's all it was: a nightmare. What if her fever had returned and this was only a hideous dream? A painful pinch of her fingers against her other arm demolished that idea. She was not only awake, but imprisoned by two unscrupulous characters and her promise to never again hurt Juli.

A few blocks from the bank, Leopold motioned for her to pull into the parking lot of a small, deserted park. "I'll drive now. Get in the back seat. Madame Zelda will sit up front."

They made the exchange.

Leopold opened his briefcase and produced a thermos bottle. When he unscrewed the cap and poured brown liquid into a cup, the delicious aroma of chocolate and cinnamon filled the car. "Drink this, then lie down."

"Go ahead, Shannon. You've always liked my Mexican chocolate," Madame Zelda told their unwilling guest.

Shannon saw mockery in the dark eyes. "You drugged me?"

The fortune-teller admitted to nothing. "How suspicious you are! Drink."

Shannon swallowed, "When pigs fly," or some other equally rude remark, and shook her head. "No, thank you." Was that steady voice really hers?

"You prefer the alternative?" Madame Zelda opened her purse and pulled out a hypodermic syringe.

Temporarily defeated, Shannon silently accepted the chocolate and drank it under their watchful eyes. She lay down, determined to stay awake, yet knowing she had no control over the present circumstances. *They didn't even blindfold me,* she thought bitterly. *That's how sure they are I won't stay awake long.* She heard the motor start, felt movement as the Honda increased speed. All too soon the familiar warmth and relaxation Shannon experienced the other times she drank Mexican chocolate stole through her. She fought against them—but lost.

Muffled voices and a feeling that something wasn't right pierced the cloud of sleep enveloping Shannon. Who were the people in her room? Why did her bed feel so hard? She slit her eyelids just enough to see rough board walls and a curtain blowing at an open window through which sunlight shone. A woodsy smell tickled her nose. Where was she?

"When she awakens, she's to write to her father and the Scott girl," a low voice said. "She's a smart one, not like some of the others. Don't give her time to think about what she's going to say or she's likely to drop in some clue."

Shannon quickly closed her eyes again.

"Not as long as she thinks we'll hurt that precious friend of hers," a woman's voice replied. "Leopold, we've got ourselves a gold mine."

Leopold! Shannon's daze lifted, but she forced herself to relax and breathe evenly. Steps came toward her. Someone picked up her hand. She let it hang like a dead salmon. After a moment, the sound of a door closing followed by silence gave her courage enough to cautiously reopen her eyes and look around her.

She lay on a rude bed in some kind of primitive cabin. A table, a chair, and some hooks on the wall evidently meant for clothing completed the furnishings.

With so much else to consider, why was she concentrating on the cabin? Fragments of the conversation made her hot and cold in turn. *"Write to her father and the Scott girl. . . Smart, not like some of the others. . . Not as long as she thinks we'll hurt that precious friend of hers."* Hope skyrocketed. Thinks? Did that mean they wouldn't hurt Juli? Her spirits fizzled, like a spent sparkler. A dreadful feeling she'd handled everything wrong grew. What if her captors had made a fool out of her and didn't intend to do anything to Juli?

"I have to get out of here," Shannon muttered. She raised her head, slipped from the hard cot on which she lay, and inched her way across the clean but unpainted board floor. A quick peek from the window showed other small cabins and a larger, more important-looking building grouped together some distance away among tall trees. Chain-link fencing surrounded the cleared area. It held back the encroaching forest, but made Shannon feel she'd been put in prison far from civilization. Singing drifted from the large building. Or was it chanting?

Realization came with the same certainty as the forest shadows already closing in on the compound. She had walked into a trap like the silly fly in the old nursery rhyme who listened to the clever spider's flattery.

# CHAPTER 12

When Juli boarded the bus the next morning, Fred Halvorsen's eyes were twin question marks. She smiled and hurried to a seat, but the smile died as soon as she sat down. She also made sure to exit in the middle of a group so he couldn't interrogate her about Shannon.

Inside Hillcrest High, the first thing Juli did was head for Amy's locker. For once, the cheerleader wasn't surrounded by boys. "Where's Shannon?"

"That's what I'd like to know." Amy pouted and childishly blew a blond curl back from her forehead. "She was supposed to pick me up."

Juli's heart lurched. Obviously Shannon hadn't stayed with Amy.

Amy went on complaining. "That's the second day in a row." Selfishness changed to genuine concern. She must care a lot more about Shannon than Juli knew. "She wasn't at school yesterday and I haven't seen her this morning. She's not sick again, is she?"

Juli's world crashed. "I—I don't think so. Sorry, but I have to run." She raced down the hall and dialed home. One finger in her ear to shut out the babble, she said, "Shannon isn't here, Dad. She didn't stay with Amy and she missed school yesterday. Doesn't this prove Mr. Halvorsen's suspicions are right?"

"Possibly. I'll get in touch with Sean right away."

"Should I come home?"

"No!" Dad's voice sharpened. "Stay out of this. I'll call the Paynes."

Juli's tense body sagged against the wall. Once she had distrusted and been suspicious of redheaded Andrew and his wife Mary. She learned to respect them after she discovered they were with the FBI. "If you need me for anything, you know where I am. Bye, Dad."

"You okay, Juli?"

She looked up into Dave Gilmore's concerned blue eyes. "No." She moistened her dry lips and whispered, "I don't know where Shannon is." The bell rang. "Tell you later."

"Wait." He gave her a quick hug. "Is there anything I can do?"

Juli blinked and started to shake her head. Then she whispered, "Pray. I'm terribly afraid Shannon is in real trouble." She turned and ran to her first class.

All day, Juli half expected Dad to come for her. He didn't. Things got worse every time someone asked about Shannon. Ted. Amy. John Foster. Molly. Mrs. Sorenson. Each time, Juli had to admit she didn't know anything. *It's true,* she fiercely defended her evasive answers. *I don't know anything. I just suspect.*

Ted was the worst. He cornered Juli between classes, eyes miserable. "Is this my fault for not handling things better that night?" he wanted to know.

Juli shook her head. "Shannon only remembers going to Burger King, then waking up with a fever. When everything settles down, you can give her a bad time about proposing." Her laugh came out sounding sick, but did bring a weak grin to Ted's lips.

"I hope Shannon gets to feeling better," Mrs. Sorenson said after class. "She promised to turn her story in yesterday. They have to be submitted by the end of the week. Yours is due, too, Juli."

"I know." She took a deep breath. "Something has come up and I haven't been able to work on it. There's no way I can finish in time to enter." The disappointment in Mrs. Sorenson's face reflected her own. "I'm really sorry."

Her teacher studied her. "It isn't the end of the world. There will be other contests." She cocked her head to one side. "I hate to bother Shannon when she's sick, but could you ask her if she has finished polishing 'Katie'? I confess I had high hopes of at least one of you placing." A shadow crossed her face. "Juli, I'm worried about Shannon. She

TROUBLE ON TUESDAY   139

isn't the same girl who came to us last fall."

"I know."

"Juli?" a masculine voice called from outside the door. Then Dave came in. "Sorry to interrupt, but if you're going to be a while, I'll go on to practice." He grinned at Mrs. Sorenson. "We need all the practice we can get, if the Pirates are going to walk off with the championship."

"We're through here. Good luck," Mrs. Sorenson told him. "Don't forget about the story, Juli."

When they stepped into the hall, Dave ordered, "Tell me about Shannon."

Juli filled him in, glad she didn't have to start at the beginning as she'd done when Dad questioned her. Dave's reaction went from startled to believing. His sunny face darkened. "It has to be that phony fortune-teller and Lord What's-his-face." He hit one fist into his other hand. "So what are we going to do? What does your dad say?"

"To stay out of it. So far, all we have is a bus driver who decided after the fact he'd seen a frightened expression on Shannon's face. You can't make a federal case out of her not waving," Juli reluctantly admitted.

"Right." Dave looked troubled. "I guess all we can do is wait." He checked his watch. "I have to go. Okay to come over tonight?"

"You'd better call me later. I don't know what's happening at home."

"See you." He loped off down the hall.

"See you," she echoed. Whoever said sharing a problem

with others cut it in two, sure knew what he or she was talking about. Juli felt pounds lighter than before talking with the other half of Scott and Gilmore, P.I.s. She took what she needed from her locker and ran outside, thrilled to find Dad waiting for her in front of the school. She slid in beside him. "Hi. What's happening?"

Gary Scott grinned with his mouth, but his gray eyes remained serious. "You'll be happy to hear Andrew and Mary are on the job. We talked with Sean and listened to the answering machine message. All it said was 'I'll be staying with a friend tonight.' Sean identified the voice as Shannon's."

"May I hear the message?" Juli pleaded.

"Yes. You might pick up on something we didn't. Besides, Sean wants to hear the whole story directly from you. He had no idea Shannon was mixed up in anything like this, but said he understood your feelings of loyalty."

"That sounds like him." Juli dreaded facing the man who always treated her like another daughter. When they reached the brick house and Sean Riley held out his arms, she flew into them. "I'm sorry."

"Of course you are." He patted her hair, gave her a lips-only smile that couldn't hide the worry in his eyes, and led her to a chair. Andrew and Mary Payne smiled encouragingly at her from the couch. "Your father has already told us the story but we'd like you to repeat it. Doing so may bring back small things you missed the first time. Do you want to talk first, or listen to the answering machine message?"

"Listen, please." She stared at the machine while Shannon's voice came strong and clear: "I'm staying with a friend tonight, Dad. See you."

What was it in the innocent words that made Juli feel uncomfortable? They certainly sounded ordinary enough. "Could I hear it again?" she asked.

Sean rewound the tape and hit Play. Juli listened, then squealed with excitement. "Got it! Shannon usually has so much expression in her voice you can tell if she's happy or sad just by her tone. This sounds like she's reading off a cereal box. There's something else, too." She closed her eyes and concentrated. "Why didn't she say 'See you tomorrow,' not just 'See you'?"

"Good question, Miss Detective." Andrew Payne grinned at her, then quickly sobered. "I listened for a pause before the word 'friend' but haven't been around Shannon enough to notice the other. Now, Juli, from the beginning. Every detail, every suspicion. I know from our previous case how observant you are."

In spite of her worry, a feeling of pride came over her. It helped clear Juli's brain of clutter, helping her to remember everything that had happened from the Tuesday Amy had brought the horoscope to school and started all the trouble. When she finished, she asked, "Now what? Do you talk with Madame Zelda and Lord Leopold?"

"No!" Andrew Payne barked. "If they're involved, the last thing we want them to know is that we suspect them."

Juli felt crushed, but cheered up when he added, "I suspect we'll get some kind of message from Shannon either this afternoon or tomorrow." He exchanged significant glances with Mary, who had stayed in the background during the interview. "Right now, we wait."

Fortunately for Juli's state of mind, the wait ended just after dinner with a sharp ring of the Scotts' telephone. She sprang to answer. "Yes? Just a moment. Dad, it's Andrew."

He took the receiver. "Hello?" A long silence followed, in which Juli thought she'd go crazy. He finally hung up. "A letter came from Shannon. The news isn't good. Andrew wants us to come over." Mom rose and started clearing the table. "Just put away the food and leave the dishes. Sean needs us."

Ten minutes later, six disturbed people sat in a circle in the Riley living room. "Andrew, will you read the letter aloud?" Sean asked. He looked ten years older than he had a few hours earlier.

"I want each of you to listen carefully," Andrew directed. "Especially you, Juli. I want your first impressions." He read aloud,

> Dear Dad,
> It's really hard to write this letter. I'm afraid you won't understand, but when a person needs some space, she should get away. You know those new friends I mentioned? I'll be staying with them. If I tell you where I am, you'll be for coming after me.

*That would defeat the whole purpose.*

*People staying here have to pay a high price. It isn't fair for others to pay one's way. I've withdrawn three hundred dollars with my cash card for the first two weeks' expenses. If you aren't willing to support this decision and put extra money in our account, you can take it from my college fund. When a person decides not to go on to school, she might as well use that money for a worthy cause.*

*I hope you will let Juli read this letter. It may help her understand why I won't be participating in the "save our streets" campaign. Everyone has to set priorities. Try not to worry too much.*

*Love, Shannon.*

"Well?" Andrew asked in a curious voice.

"It sounds as if Shannon means it," Sean replied, face chalky.

Juli leaped from her chair, her eyes wide. "No!" She grabbed the paper, too excited to be polite. "Every sentence can be taken two ways. Whoever kidnapped her and made her write the letter won't catch on in a million years, but it's loaded with subtle clues she knew I'd recognize."

Andrew grunted. Juli couldn't tell whether he agreed or was testing her. "Listen to it again, but read between the lines," she urged. "Shannon says it's really hard to write this letter and she's afraid her dad won't understand. Then she goes into this stuff about 'a person' needing space and getting away. She doesn't say one word about her wanting to get away."

"So?" Mary Payne's question snapped like a hungry trout at a fly.

"Fact: Shannon is an A student in writing. Fact: Mrs. Sorenson is death on adding editorial-type comments and generalizations. Shannon uses them all the way through." Juli scanned the page. "She says it isn't fair for others to pay 'one's' way. And when 'a person' decides not to go on to school, she 'might'—the word should be 'may'—as well use the money for a worthy cause. 'Everyone has to set priorities.' Another generalization."

Dad peered over her shoulder. "Good work, honey. Anything else?"

"Yes." Juli grew more and more excited. "She doesn't say Sean's coming for her would defeat her purpose, but 'the' purpose. She says can instead of may. Mrs. Sorenson would flunk Shannon if she turned in this kind of work. I don't get the 'save our streets' stuff. We never even discussed the program. Maybe it's so Sean would make sure I read the letter?"

"Wrong," Andrew stated. "The first letters spell SOS."

"The universal distress signal!" Mom gasped.

"We know one thing," Andrew pointed out. "Even if Shannon had been given drugs, she knew what she was doing when she wrote that letter. "

All Juli's happiness fled. "I'd rather we'd just find her."

"We will. I promise." His steady gaze helped settle Juli down. "The letter was mailed yesterday at Deming, about fifteen miles northeast of here on the way to Mount Baker. Ring any bells?"

Something stirred in Juli's consciousness. She tried to capture the tantalizing thought that hovered just out of reach.

"If only I could remember," she told Clue that night, then said her prayers. "I can't help feeling it's important, God," she prayed. "Please, help me remember."

Andrew had reluctantly agreed Juli should tell Shannon's closest friends she'd gone away, so they wouldn't worry. "Just say she's been under a lot of pressure," he directed. Amy immediately wanted to know if she were to blame for taking Shannon to Madame Zelda and going with her to the Children of Light meetings.

"At first I went for fun," she said. "Then it got boring. Shannon gave me a bunch of literature about a weekend retreat in the woods and felt bad when I told her I didn't want to go." She changed the subject. "I can't wait for the play-offs!"

A bell pealed inside Juli's head, loud and clear. She stared at Amy, remembering her chatter weeks ago about a retreat and saying the Children of Light had grounds near Mount Baker. Even Juli's toes tingled. Just maybe. . .

A private conference with Ted ended with his promising to find and bring the literature, if Amy hadn't tossed it.

He eyed Juli suspiciously. "This has something to do with Shannon, doesn't it? You aren't considering going, are you?"

"I need to have you trust me, okay?" He nodded, but Juli silently thanked God for what might be a much-needed break. She also pushed her luck. "Any chance of dropping it by if you do find it?"

"Dave said he's going to your place tonight. He can bring it." Ted started off. "Juli, if anything happens to Shannon. . ." His voice died away.

All the prayers on her friend's behalf made Juli say, "Things are rough right now, but I can't help feeling she will be just fine. Keep believing it, Ted."

"I'm trying," he said huskily. This time he didn't stop or look back.

She boarded the bus, said hello to Fred Halvorsen, and wished they could return to the ham-and-eggs days. Juli knew Andrew Payne had questioned the driver. Now he greeted her with raised eyebrows, but she could only shake her head. Each time, Juli saw the same sadness in his eyes she carried in her heart.

Dave arrived shortly after dinner. "Present, Juli." He dropped a sealed envelope into her eager hands. "My best friend's not writing secret love letters to my girlfriend, is he?"

Juli blushed. "Of course not. It's information on the retreat Amy mentioned."

"Are we going?" He sounded innocent enough, but his eyes twinkled.

"I'd be grounded for life if I even suggested it! Let's go to the living room. Dad and Mom went for a walk and I need to talk before they get back."

"You sound mysterious. Have you learned something more about Shannon?"

"Andrew and Mary Payne are investigating." Juli slit open the envelope and took out a flyer on the retreat. It had a rough sketch of a few cabins and what looked like a dining or meeting hall set in trees. "Doesn't look like much."

"Is the chain-link fence around the compound to keep people out or in?"

Juli shivered. "It's really isolated looking. Do you think Shannon's there?"

"Why don't Andrew and Mary and your dad search the compound and see?"

"To get a warrant, they have to convince a judge there's evidence of a crime, and probable cause for the search. They just don't have it."

"That wouldn't prevent their doing surveillance, would it?" he asked bluntly.

Juli's mouth curved into a smile. "No, and when they see this flyer, that's exactly what I'm hoping they will do!"

# CHAPTER 13

Juli described the days that followed Shannon's disappearance as, "worst of times, worst of times." Dark clouds of despair followed each ray of hope. Every up had a down, each lower than the one before.

Andrew Payne asked Juli to go through Shannon's wardrobe. Her red ski jacket, heavy shoes, and warm clothing were missing. Juli's hopes rose. Fred Halvorsen had been positive Shannon was wearing the ski jacket that Monday.

Juli also found Shannon's story, "Katie," neatly printed out and ready for Mrs. Sorenson. She asked Sean's permission to turn it in. "If, I mean *when* she gets back, she'll be glad to know it was entered in the contest," Juli said. Sean nodded and turned away, but not before Juli saw the grief he couldn't hide.

Ryan Riley left the running of Skagit House to his capable staff and came in to stay with his son. White-haired and with blue-gray eyes so like Shannon's it made Juli want to cry, just having Grand with them raised everyone's spirits. The fact of his granddaughter's absence had temporarily erased his blarney, but not his brogue. "Our Father (it sounded like fey-ther) will not be for lettin' harm come to our Irish colleen," he stated firmly.

Juli wished she could be as sure. She had come even closer to God through prayer, and found comfort from studying her Bible more than ever before, especially the Psalms. She fought off anxiety by keeping as busy as possible. It wasn't difficult, with all the things happening at home and school.

In spite of the Pirates' best efforts, the team was defeated early in the basketball play-offs. Coach told the student body, "Next year will be a different story. Most of our starting lineup will be back. We'll bring home the trophy!" His positive attitude took away some of the disappointment of losing.

The Monday following the one when Shannon vanished, Sean received a second letter from Shannon. This one was postmarked Acme, another small town between Bellingham and Mount Baker. Shannon wrote that she'd be away indefinitely. It also said, "I maxed out our joint account. The price of staying here is even higher than I thought." She repeated that he could transfer money from her college fund, and closed with, "Please ask Juli to tell everyone hi, especially Katie and her sister. They'd fit right in here."

"They must be very sure Shannon has convinced me she's joined them of her own free will," Sean bitterly remarked. "I wonder if they took her to a cash machine, or if she gave them the PIN (personal identification number)."

"If they're actually using the card, you can bet they will be wearing gloves," Gary Scott said, looking grim. "No way will they leave prints that may incriminate them. By the way, how much was in the account?"

"More than $1,200." Sean paused, then asked, "What should I do about adding more? If I don't, will they hurt her?"

"I suggest you wait a few days," Dad advised. "The $1,500 they already have should satisfy them for a while."

*Was Dad just a bit too casual?* Juli wondered. Suspicion constantly simmered beneath the surface of her mind. Now it bubbled up and over. Dad had been tight-lipped ever since she turned over the flyer for the Children of Light retreat. If she asked him a question, he brushed her off like a pesky mosquito, or promptly changed the subject. She knew from long years as a police officer's daughter how little of his work could be shared with his family, but stubbornly resisted his silence. Shannon was her best friend. Having to stand by doing nothing was the hardest thing Juli had ever been forced to endure.

"Who are Katie and her sister?" Dad asked.

"They aren't real," Juli explained. "Katie is both the

title and heroine of Shannon's contest entry. She and her little sister go through terrible hardships during the Irish potato famine. Shannon's saying they'd fit right in where she is has to be a clue showing how bad things really are."

"Good thinking, Juli. Every little thing helps build our case."

Juli sighed. At this rate, Shannon would be an old woman before they rescued her from Lord Leopold and Madame Zelda! At least there was one bright spot. Dave had finished basketball practice for the year and they could spend more time together. Instead of riding the bus home from school, Juli climbed into his Mustang, aware of envious looks from many of the girls.

"Why don't we do some sleuthing on our own?" he asked one sunny afternoon. "I don't mean anything that will interfere with your dad or the Paynes. Just minor stuff, like driving by a few special places." His eyes gleamed.

Juli sat bolt upright in her seat. "Like a certain fortune-teller's house?"

"Bingo." A big grin broke open his face. "There's no reason Madame Zelda would know me. I wasn't that close to her at the surprise party. What's her address? Oh, and . . .is there any way you can look different? The odds are ten to one she's made it her business to know you!"

"She's in the phone book." Juli dug in her backpack, hoping to find a scrunchie or baseball cap, anything to disguise herself. "We'll have to stop at a store, one with a phone booth."

"Okay." He put the car in gear and headed for the nearest shopping center.

Fifteen minutes later, Juli caught her hair up with a scrunchie and shoved it under a baseball cap pulled down to eyes hidden by dark glasses. Dave laughed. "All right! When we get there, scoot down in the seat and look short."

Juli pulled down the sun visor on her side and looked in the mirror. "Just call me Mata Hari, female spy."

"She was wicked. You aren't," Dave teased. "You don't want to end up like she did. The French executed her for being a German spy during World War I."

"Oops." Juli giggled. It felt good. There hadn't been much laughter in her life lately. Her high spirits, born from feeling they were finally doing something toward solving the case, lasted all the way to Madame Zelda's house. The curtains were open, but they saw no sign of the exotic fortune-teller.

"I could pretend to be a client and go in," Dave volunteered.

"Not a bad idea, but let's keep it as a last resort. Right now, it might do more harm than good," Juli told him. A feeling of urgency rushed through her. "Dave, please take me to the Hiltons. Ted may know where the Children of Light hold their meetings. I don't want Amy to know we're asking, unless she absolutely has to. She talks too much."

"Right." He headed away from Madame Zelda's and toward the Hiltons'.

To Juli's relief, Ted was home but not Amy. He also knew where the group met. "I followed Shannon once," he sheepishly admitted. "Couldn't get it out of my head that she and Amy were getting mixed up with a bunch of crazies. Let's get going." When they looked surprised, an obstinate look came over his face. "It's time you let me in on this. Shannon's my girl, isn't she?"

Dave drove through late afternoon traffic to the downtown area. He and Juli explained on the way that Shannon might have gone somewhere with the Children of Light. They didn't add she might have gone unwillingly. Juli had already sworn Dave to secrecy concerning the bus driver's observations and Shannon's letters.

"I hope not," Ted groaned. He directed them to an unpretentious building among a dozen others. "I don't know which room. There must be a list inside."

The three friends stepped into a tiled-floor lobby. A large directory hung near an elevator. They scanned the listings. "Funny, I know this is the building." Ted stared at the directory. "I don't see Children of Light."

Juli's stomach twisted. "There's a blank space next to 304. Do you think—?"

"We'd better check it out." Dave pushed the elevator's UP button. The short, silent ride felt an eternity long. The door to suite 304 stood open. Humming sounds came from within. Dave pushed in front of Juli and all three stepped inside.

One look shattered their hopes. The lone occupant wore

blue coveralls. Except for him, his whirring vacuum cleaner, and a cleaning cart, the room was empty. Glimpses through open doors into the rest of the suite showed all the rooms were deserted.

Dave walked over to the cleaner. "Excuse me?"

The man looked up, smiled, and obligingly turned off his vacuum. "Yes?"

"The people who used this room. The Children of Light. Where are they?"

"When I came this afternoon, the building superintendent told me they had gone and to clean for the next occupants." He looked at them curiously.

"Do you know where they went?" Dave asked.

"No. The superintendent might. He's in the office on the first floor."

They thanked him and rode back downstairs. Dave gave Juli a meaningful look. "Do you want to wait in the car?" His look added it was better that way, in case Lord Leopold came back to see if anyone had inquired about him.

"All right." She slowly walked out and crawled into the Mustang.

Five minutes later, they joined her. "Their lease doesn't end until May first, but they cleared out during the night. The superintendent found a note dropped in his mail slot. They didn't ask for a return on their rent or leave a forwarding address." Dave took Juli's hand. "He also asked why all the sudden interest."

Ted put in from the back seat, "Dave mumbled we

wanted to get in touch with one of the members—do we ever!—and the superintendent grunted. He started to say something, then shut his mouth. We thanked him and split. We must not be the only ones asking about the Children of Light."

Juli felt as though she were breaking inside. Bands of fear tightened around her and made it hard to breathe. Somehow she managed to act natural until they dropped Ted off, then turned to Dave in a panic. "What does it mean?"

"I don't know. Are you going to tell your dad and the Paynes what we did?"

Juli stared out the window. "No. They have to be the ones who checked. There's nothing else we can do except keep waiting." She added around the lump in her throat, "And praying."

Less than a hundred miles away, Madame Zelda rudely yanked Shannon Riley from one nightmare to another. "Get up," she commanded harshly. "We're getting you out of here. Someone's been watching us." She shoved Shannon's ski jacket and a blanket at her. "Don't take time to dress."

Shannon was too dazed to obey. She cringed when Lord Leopold cursed, picked her up, and carried her outside. He dumped her into the back seat of a car with its motor running. Was it her Honda? Confused and exhausted, Shannon didn't struggle. If only she could sleep! She clutched the blanket around her and collapsed in a heap. Once she roused enough to realize she'd been transferred to a different vehicle, harder riding than her own, then slept again.

Just before daylight, Shannon awoke on her hard cot. Head still fuzzy, she wondered if she had dreamed it all? If not, why had she been spirited away, then returned? She dared not ask. Although her two meals a day were served in her cabin, Shannon had been allowed to walk daily in the compound and attend services that soon deteriorated to wild ravings and shouts of submission from the Children of Light.

"Those present who refuse to acknowledge me as their protector and savior will be cut off and never see God," Lord Leopold thundered over and over. He quoted Scriptures to prove his point, rattling them off like a hail of bullets. The only way Shannon kept her sanity was to close her eyes, sway as if listening intently, and mentally repeat Bible verses she had learned at her mother's knee. When the white-robed leader's voice threatened to drown them out, she clung to a few words from the twenty-third Psalm: "I will fear no evil: for Thou art with me."

Those ten words became a lifeline. Shannon quoted them in her heart and mind a hundred, perhaps a thousand times. They kept her from giving in to the hypnotic effect of Lord Leopold. They helped her fight off the choking smell of those around her smoking grass, many far younger than she. They kept hope and faith alive long after it should have died. Hope that Juli had understood the clues Shannon worked out while she pretended to be unconscious. Faith that God would deliver her, as He once delivered the children of Israel from bondage.

Shannon had already confessed her sin of allowing Amy, then her own needs, to lead her into temptation. She felt like the person in a story who said, "Please, God, forgive my sin," then rejoiced when God replied, "What sin, my child?" God had forgiven and forgotten her sin, although she hadn't!

Two days earlier, everything had changed. Shannon was no longer allowed outside. Lord Leopold carried on his conversion sermons in private sessions until she wondered how long she could hold out. Outwardly obedient, angry inside, Shannon wrote the second letter to her father and surrendered her cash card to Madame Zelda. Why didn't someone come for her? It had been nine days since they brought her here. Or was it eight? Or ten? She couldn't remember.

Shannon refused to drink chocolate and ate only enough food to keep from starving. It was easy enough to say she wasn't hungry at the time and could eat it later. She could, even though she wouldn't. Fearing it might contain drugs, she burned it in the stove that warmed the cabin.

She could not continue like this. Shannon knew she had three choices: escape now, before her growing weakness destroyed the possibility; eat the food served her, even though it probably was drugged; or die. She'd learned earlier her captors never bothered to lock the door. "Because they think I'm drugged," she whispered.

She dressed and stepped outside. The compound stretched before her, deathly still. Not a leaf whispered. Not a branch stirred. No birds sang.

Scarcely daring to breathe, Shannon crept across the murky space that felt like a mile. She reached the gate in the chain-link fence. Hope died. A strong padlock kept the world out, the Children of Light in. She could never climb the fence in her poor condition. A slight rustle in the bushes brought her heart to her throat. Was the compound guarded day and night? If she were caught, what would happen to her? She backed away and sobbed with relief when she saw a small brown rabbit hop from beneath one bush to another.

Dizzy from the exertion, Shannon stole back to her cabin and curled up on the cot. Her choices had dwindled to two: eat drugged food or die.

About the same time Shannon tried to escape, Juli crouched outside the partly open door of the Scott den. Fear for Shannon overcame guilt for eavesdropping after the ring of the phone shattered the early morning hush. Moments later, appalled by the story Dad's questions and responses told, Juli made it back to her room undetected and grabbed a notebook. She didn't dare turn on a light. When she heard Dad go back to bed, she wrote the chilling facts:

1. *A surveillance crew had been observing the Children of Light compound.*

2. *They made a map of the complete area: buildings, trees, everything.*

3. *They briefly glimpsed a dark-haired girl in a red ski jacket.*

4. *They watched food being taken to an isolated cabin at ten A.M.. and six P.M.*

5. *They observed people gathering for some kind of meeting in a big hall.*

6. *They heard singing, ranting and raving, and smelled marijuana smoke.*

7. *A county judge agreed it could be a kidnapping and issued a search warrant specifically naming all grounds inside the fence and each building.*

8. *Lord Leopold personally accompanied them on the search. He admitted Shannon had been there, but insisted she came and left of her own free will.*

9. *The search team didn't find Shannon. They did find a filthy red jacket, but it was obviously too small to be hers.*

10. *They found no trace of Shannon's Honda.*

"It adds up to one big, fat nothing, God," Juli whispered. "Now what?" Her conversation with Dave in front of

Madame Zelda's house beat at her brain and rang in her ears. Dave: *"I could pretend to be a client."* Her own voice: *"We'll save it for a last resort."* The search had failed. It was time for desperate action.

# CHAPTER 14

Dave Gilmore planned to tackle Madame Zelda with the same thoroughness he used to solve tough math problems. First, he would need to make her trust him and invite him to the retreat so he could check out the compound. Second, she mustn't connect him with Juli. He promptly called the fortune-teller, made an appointment, then took drastic steps toward changing his appearance.

Juli nearly freaked when he showed up almost bald and with his remaining hair dyed black. "You aren't even the same Dave Gilmore!"

"You're looking at David Allen," he told her. "I'll use my middle name when I infiltrate the Children of Light. Now that the compound's been searched, they'll consider it the safest place to keep her. She's probably being drugged, so I'll need help getting her out. Your dad and the Paynes can't be in on a snatch. We have to clue Ted and John in."

"I just hope we're doing the right thing." Juli's voice sounded small.

"We're out of options," Dave reminded, blue eyes steady. "Don't worry about me. I'm not going to do anything stupid." Yet, a few days later, when he parked John Foster's VW bug—another precaution—in front of Madame Zelda's, Dave shot up a quick prayer for help, even though the white-clad woman didn't look like a fanatic. "Thanks for seeing me," he told her. "Like I said on the phone, Amy Hilton mentioned you. I know she quit coming, but that's Amy."

"Is your problem serious?" Her warm voice was like syrup.

Dave thought of Shannon and his voice hardened. "Life stinks right now and it's getting worse." *No acting about that.* "My girlfriend tells me I'm not even the same person. My folks and sister bug me." *About my hair.* "Should a guy just let everyone dump on him? How come people don't understand when you need to get away?" Would Madame Zelda swallow his phony baloney?

"You were wise to come to me, David. Would you like hot chocolate and some pastry before we talk?"

"Thanks, but I had a huge lunch. Anyway, I'm not supposed to have too much chocolate." *Especially yours,* he mentally added.

Something flickered in her dark eyes, but Madame

Zelda gracefully beckoned him to follow her down the hall. He recognized the barren room from what Shannon had told Juli. The theatrical setting made him want to laugh. How could anyone believe in this stuff? *Shannon's future may depend on my acting ability,* Dave warned himself. "Interesting," he said.

"It is useful in helping one relax." Madame Zelda sat down across from him and placed her hands on the crystal ball. "You are unhappy, David," she said in a trancelike tone. "You need not be. The Creator of the universe longs for you to find peace. Those around you do not understand. Many others do. Their number is growing. Are you willing to open yourselves to the spirit's leadings?"

"Oh, yes!" Dave told her. He silently added: *the Holy Spirit.* A chill chased through him. Madame Zelda was far more dangerous than he and Juli had thought. Coupled with drugged chocolate, the woman with half-closed eyes whose voice went on and on could have a powerful influence on a troubled person's mind.

"Then all will be well. I see you in the midst of a group of those who suffer as you do. They will bring you great joy. You must not be afraid to walk in the light. Leaving those who hold you back may prove to be painful for a time, but the end will be glorious. David Allen, you are special. You did not come here on your own. You were sent, that you might learn to do great things."

Dave nearly choked. He bowed his head as if overcome with emotion. "I don't know how to thank you," he said in a husky voice. "You have helped me more than you know." He looked up and put on his most innocent expression. "How can I find the others like me, those who don't know where to turn?"

Madame Zelda raised her gaze from the crystal ball to Dave's face. "Go home. Examine your heart. If you decide your family and friends no longer meet your needs, come see me tomorrow. Meanwhile, I will consult the spirits."

Three sessions later, "David Allen" received a flyer inviting him to be part of a special weekend retreat in a wooded area near Mount Baker. He came home from it both ecstatic and disturbed. "The place was crawling with kids our age," he told Juli, Ted, and John. "They're either rebellious or from rotten homes. They really lapped up all Lord Leopold's talk about love, acceptance, and being one big family. He's good. I'll give him that. If I didn't have a terrific home, parents, and God, he might even convince me! Just kidding," he quickly added.

"What about drugs?"

Dave shook his head. "Zip, except for maybe in the Mexican chocolate. Hope the birds and squirrels don't get bombed. I dumped mine in the bushes."

"Who cares about all that stuff?" Juli cried. "What about Shannon?"

"I didn't see her, but there's a small cabin off from the others. I asked what it was. Madame Zelda told me it's for those who need time and privacy to resolve conflict of mind and soul. The person stays alone, prays, and meditates. Someone takes meals to the cabin." Dave pulled a crudely drawn map from his pocket. Four heads bent over the sketch of cabins, trees, bushes, and fence.

"I suspect the gate is normally padlocked. This time it stayed open, probably to show people are free to come and go. Leopold came down heavy on being separate. He asked those who might want to be part of the Children of Light to stand at the last service. Most of us did. Leopold promised to notify those he feels are ready to leave all and follow the Master. 'Master' as in him, I'll bet.

"I told him afterwards I'd give anything to feel peace." Dave's eyes were somber. "I would, because of Shannon. I begged to be allowed to come during spring vacation when Dad, Mom, and Christy will be gone." His grin chased the shadows away. "I guarantee I'll be one of the chosen few. I made sure to let it slip my dad was driving a brand-new BMW. He is, but it's a company car!"

Laughter spread through the group. It ended when Juli asked, "Now what?"

"We need to plan a way to make contact if I'm inside," Dave told them. "If I do join the Children of Light, I can't be sure they won't ask for my watch and other worldly possessions." He looked at the map again. "Lord Leopold mentioned they have nightly meetings in the large building. There's heavy shrubbery inside and outside the chain-link fence, especially the southwest corner. Ted, John, I'll meet you there on Friday night, as soon as it gets good and dark." He looked sternly at Juli. "Not you. It could wreck everything."

"Will we take Shannon out then?" Ted asked, worry all over his face. The Washington State Patrol had notified Sean Riley the day before that they'd found Shannon's Honda abandoned many miles away from the Children of Light camp.

"I don't know, but bring flashlights and wire cutters. If she's there, we can't take her out the gate. If she's drugged, we'll have to carry her."

Juli stammered, "Wh-what if they drug *you?* You might get pulled into the cult, like Shannon did." She bit her lip. "There haven't been any more letters."

"It's a chance we have to take," Dave said. "Look. God doesn't want Shannon caught in a cult. He's going to be on the job. Hang in there, okay?"

Armed with prayer and a supply of granola bars, David Allen Gilmore put on the performance of his life during spring vacation week. He caught a bus to Madame Zelda's after she sent word he could come. Dave handed her a soiled hundred dollar bill. "Camps need money," he told her. "But this is all I have right now. The VW was borrowed. I've been talking with Dad about cars, but now. . ." He shrugged. "Maybe I can make up for it in other ways. I'm willing to do whatever it takes to show people how important it is to love and follow God."

His bold move and sincerity disarmed Madame Zelda, and when they reached the compound, Lord Leopold. If they had cherished schemes to extort money from Dave's father who drove the BMW, they dropped them. Their excitement over the seemingly dedicated convert grew. No one at the compound was more willing to enthusiastically testify to the power of God's love. The cult leaders didn't know Dave spent hours praying. If only something he said could penetrate the marijuana smoke and reach one of the brainwashed kids! He devoured granola bars to avoid eating much of the food, just in case.

On Friday night, Dave crouched in the shrubs at the southwest corner of the compound. Heart racing, he talked to Ted and John, hidden outside the fence. "Shannon's here. I saw her through the door when they took her food. She looks bad. She won't be able to help herself." He ignored Ted's low groan and went on. "They don't lock the cabin door, so there have to be drugs in her food."

"How are we going to get her out?" John whispered. "And when?"

"Early morning. Make a hole in the fence back here big enough for us to get Shannon through in a hurry. Do it during the meeting. The singing and yelling will cover any noise you make. Ted, be ready to crawl through when I come for you. Shannon will be drugged from supper, maybe sick. We'll do the best we can to take care of her. By morning she will be as free from the drugs as she'll get. We have to be out of here before daylight. John, where's the Mustang?"

"Hidden about a mile from here."

Dave clenched his sweaty hands. "Good. Turn the car around so it will be headed away from camp. When you see a flashlight blink twice, back up."

"I will." John Foster's steady, dependable voice steadied Dave's nerves. When John said he'd be there, he'd be there.

"I have to be inside before the meeting ends." Dave hesitated, then whispered, "One other thing. Pray. We're going to need all the help we can get."

Dave made it back inside without anyone noticing his absence. He joined in the clamor and swayed with the others while Lord Leopold worked himself into a frenzy. Even in his short stay at the compound, Dave had realized the physical price such high-pitched emotion demanded. Sometimes the worshipers, if anyone in his right mind could call them that, fell into an exhausted sleep before leaving the large building. Others staggered to their quarters and became sodden heaps.

Tonight was no different. Dave, fully dressed beneath his blanket, waited long enough to be sure his cabinmates slept. He longed to fill his lungs with good night air and rid himself of the stench of marijuana. At last he rose. Shoes in hand, he stole out, freezing each time a board creaked or someone turned over. He located Ted and signaled for him to follow.

What felt like a century later, he and Ted reached Shannon's cabin and peered in the window. Silence. They stepped inside. The long, dark form on the cot didn't move.

Ted dimmed a flashlight with his shirt and risked a quick look.

Shannon lay on the outside of a blanket, wearing a wrinkled sweatshirt and jeans. Tousled black hair made her face ghostlike. She breathed so softly the boys leaned close to make sure she was alive. Dave hissed in Ted's ear, "I have a funny feeling we need to get out of here. Now!"

Ted sounded sick when he whispered back, "We can't take a chance on Shannon moaning when we move her. Do you have something to gag her?" Dave silently handed Ted a handkerchief, too angry at the wicked leaders who made such a thing necessary, to speak. "Grab her shoes and jacket, but don't try to get them on her," he warned. "Leave everything else. Come on!"

"God, please help us," Ted muttered half under his breath.

Dave gripped his friend's hand. What if it were Juli, helpless and trapped? "Shannon won't be here much longer," he grimly vowed. "I'll take her shoulders. You take her feet. She's totally out of it." They staggered to the opening in the chain-link fence and got through. Two quick flashes of light brought John with the Mustang. He jumped out and helped steady Shannon while Ted crawled into the crowded back seat, then they handed her limp body to him. "You drive," Dave told John. "I'm beat." He gulped in great breaths of air.

John no sooner stepped on the gas than a shout came from the compound. The poison of fear filled the car. No need for silence now. John jammed the gas pedal to the floor. The car shot forward and roared down the road. Ted carefully removed the gag from Shannon's mouth. Dave kept his head turned to watch for pursuers. None came. Once off the back roads, John sped up. "Bellingham hospital?"

"Right." Dave's muscles slowly unkinked. Yet every time lights flashed in the rearview mirror, he tensed until the vehicle passed or fell back. A lifetime later, they turned Shannon over to Emergency Room personnel and faced a barrage of questions. "We can't answer until we contact her father and Gary Scott," Dave protested. "Can you get Dr. Marlowe? She has Shannon's medical history."

"Juli." An unwelcome voice shattered her sleep of worry and exhaustion.

She opened her eyes. "Dad? What's wrong?" Terrified at the set look around his mouth, Juli sprang out of bed and grabbed his arm. "Is it Mom?"

"No. Dave Gilmore called. Shannon's in the hospital. Get up and dress."

Sleep fled. Juli clutched at Dad's arm and cried, "Is she all right?"

"He thinks so. Hurry." Gary Scott broke free and stalked out the door.

Juli's shaking hands got her into jeans and a sweater. Comb in hand, she ran toward the hall and her parents' voices. "I'm ready. What else did Dave say?"

"He infiltrated the Children of Light. Ted Hilton and John Foster helped him get Shannon away from the compound. What do you know about this?"

She shivered at his icy voice. "Everything."

"I appreciate your honesty. We'll talk later." Dad swung into the parking lot.

"Later" turned out to be after two or three eternities. Dr. Marlowe arrived, checked Shannon, and bluntly told the concerned group of Scotts, Rileys, and the three boys, "There's no sign of physical abuse. She's dropped a good ten pounds and is weak. She's obviously been given some type of drug. I've ordered blood tests."

"Is she going to be all right?" Juli dug her nails into her hands until it hurt.

Dr. Marlowe hesitated, and Juli's heart shot to her throat. She wondered if it had parked there permanently when the unsmiling doctor said, "I'm less concerned about Shannon's physical condition than I am the mental and emotional trauma she has experienced. I'll know better when I can talk with her."

The doctor glanced around the circle and addressed Gary Scott. "I can tell you this, even before a more thorough examination that has to wait until Shannon is conscious and her body drug-free. These boys acted rashly. They took a terrible risk. They may also have saved her life. I suspect Shannon Riley came as near to the breaking point as any person can and still keep her sanity."

Juli's traitorous stomach sent her flying to the closest

restroom. This time it was Mom who wiped her hot face and held her close. "Go ahead and cry. Shannon will need you when she wakes up." Juli clung to her mother, praying she could be strong enough to help her friend through the hard days ahead.

All night long, Sean and Grand Riley kept silent vigil by Shannon's bedside. Dad took Mom and Juli home, saying, "You'll be needed more tomorrow." Hours after she tumbled into bed, Saturday afternoon sunlight sneaked in Juli's window and awakened her. The whole sickening mess returned.

"Mom? Dad?" She bolted from bed and ran toward the sound of voices in the kitchen. A broadly grinning Gary Scott was on the phone. Even before he hung up, Juli knew he had good news. "Thank God! Sean says Shannon's awake and asking for you, Juli. She's far more alert than Dr. Marlowe expected."

"Yes!" Juli made a dive to get dressed, impatiently stuffed down a sandwich, and talked nonstop all the way to Shannon's hospital room. Grand and Sean Riley smiled at her from the foot of the bed. Mom and Dad stayed in the doorway. Juli stared at Shannon. Except for being pale, she looked normal. She sounded normal, too, when she sat up and held out her arms. "Where's my hug?"

Juli just about lost it. She stumbled across the spotless room and put her arms around the Irish girl whose merry smile couldn't completely hide the shadows lurking in her blue-gray eyes. "I am so glad you're, uh, back!" She couldn't bring herself to say "all right." Dr. Marlowe had said Shannon would need counseling, perhaps even deprogramming, before her damaged body, mind, and spirit could heal.

Andrew and Mary Payne arrived a short time later to hear Shannon's story. Juli and the boys were allowed to be present. Juli had to blink hard when Shannon told how the only thing that kept her going was repeating the ten words: "I will fear no evil: for Thou art with me."

"To think you were there, and I didn't even know," she exclaimed when she learned of Dave, Ted, and John's daring rescue. Her courage slipped. "They won't come back for me, will they?"

"No," Andrew Payne told her. "After I learned you were here, we sent a team to the compound. The Children of Light are gone. I suspect they cleared out immediately after realizing you were missing. I wouldn't be surprised if they turned up in Canada. As far as you're concerned, Shannon, it's over."

"Then I'm free." Tears replaced the shadows in her eyes. "Free as an eagle!"

Juli started to say, "Free as a bird, not an eagle." No. This was Shannon's moment to soar. Not even her best friend had the right to ground her.

**Books for ages 7 to 12**

# Kid Stuff
*Fun-filled Activity Books*
*for ages 7-12*

### Bible Questions and Answers for Kids
### Collection #1 and #2

Brain-teasing questions and answers from the Bible are sure to sat-
isfy the curiosity of any kid. And fun illustrations combined with
Bible trivia make for great entertainment and learning! Trade
paper; 8 ½" x 11" $2.97 each.

### Bible Crosswords for Kids
### Collection #1 and #2

Two great collections of Bible-based crossword puzzles are sure to
challenge kids ages seven to twelve. Hours of enjoyment and Bible
learning are combined into these terrific activity books. Trade
paper; 8 ½" x 11" $2.97 each.

### The Kid's Book of Awesome Bible Activities
### Collection #1 and #2

These fun-filled, Bible-based activity books include challenging
word searches, puzzles, hidden pictures, and more! Bible learning
becomes fun and meaningful with *The Kid's Book of Awesome
Bible Activities*. Trade paper; 8 ½" x 11" $2.97 each.

---

## Available wherever books are sold.
### Or order from:
Barbour & Company, Inc.
P.O. Box 719
Uhrichsville, Ohio 44683
http://www.barbourbooks.com

If you order by mail, add $2.00 to your order for shipping. Prices subject to
change without notice.